Computer Crunch!

Patricia Barnes-Svarney

Published by POCKET BOOKS
New York London Toronto Sydney Tokyo Singapore

This book is a work of fiction. Names, characters, places and incidents are products of the author's imagination or are used fictitiously. Any resemblance to actual events or locales or persons, living or dead, is entirely coincidental.

A MINSTREL PAPERBACK *Original*

A Minstrel Book published by
POCKET BOOKS, a division of Simon & Schuster Inc.
1230 Avenue of the Americas, New York, NY 10020

ISBN: 0-671-01884-1

First Minstrel Books printing February 1998

10 9 8 7 6 5 4 3 2 1

Cover photography by Pat Hill Studio and Danny Feld

Printed in the U.S.A.

Welcome to the Secret World of Alex Mack!

I thought working on a class newsletter without the help of computers would be a fun, challenging project. Instead, it's turning into a major competition. My group is trying to put together a good paper, but the other newsletter group keeps scooping our stories. Is someone spying on me again? And have they seen me use my powers? Let me explain. . . .

I'm Alex Mack. I was just another average kid until my first day of junior high.

One minute I'm walking home from school—the next there's a *crash!* A truck from the Paradise Valley Chemical plant overturns in front of me, and I'm drenched in some weird chemical.

And since then—well, nothing's been the same. I can move objects with my mind, shoot electrical charges through my fingertips, and morph into a liquid shape . . . which is handy when I get in a tight spot!

My best friend, Ray, thinks it's cool—and my sister, Annie, thinks I'm a science project.

They're the only two people who know about my new powers. I can't let anyone else find out—not even my parents—because I know the chemical plant wants to find me and turn me into some experiment.

But you know something? I guess I'm not so average anymore!

The Secret World of Alex Mack™

Alex, You're Glowing!
Bet You Can't!
Bad News Babysitting!
Witch Hunt!
Mistaken Identity!
Cleanup Catastrophe!
Take a Hike!
Go for the Gold!
Poison in Paradise!
Zappy Holidays! (Super Edition)
Junkyard Jitters!
Frozen Stiff!
I Spy!
High Flyer!
Milady Alex!
Father-Daughter Disaster!
Bonjour, Alex!
Close Encounters!
Hocus Pocus!
Halloween Invaders!
Truth Trap!
New Year's Revolution! (Super Edition)
Lost in Vegas!
Computer Crunch!

Available from MINSTREL Books

To Junior, who started it all. . . .

Computer Crunch!

CHAPTER 1

Dear Annie,

I never thought I'd be writing to you through the e-mail. It's probably better—I think Mom was mad about the last phone bill. You know, the day I called you to ask where you put your tennis racket. (I still can't find it and Ray still wants to borrow it) . . . By the way, did you say you had a list of those e-mail things? Louis was telling me that "smile" in e-mail is :), and that smile with a beard is :)> Did I do that right? (It's supposed to be like a face on its side, right?) . . . Ray says hi and wants to know if you would buy him a T-shirt so he

can brag about your school . . . Mom wants the laptop all the time for her homework and Dad won't spring for a new computer. Uh oh. I think I hear someone coming. Probably after the computer . . . Love, Alex

"Oh, Alex."

Alex Mack thought she heard a soft voice calling her name. It seemed so distant she really couldn't tell. Shrugging her shoulders, she adjusted her CD player's headphones and turned up the volume as one of her favorite songs came on.

"Alex," she heard again, a little more insistent now. Alex fidgeted in her chair, then leaned closer to the laptop computer screen on her desk, trying to concentrate. She just *had* to send this message to her older sister, Annie. After all, Ray had been bugging her for days about the tennis racket and the T-shirt. *Maybe if I just pretend I don't hear anything the voice will go away,* she thought, clicking the computer mouse button to send the message.

As the computer beeped in response to sending the electronic mail, something caught Alex's eye. Barbara Mack, Alex's mother, had picked up a dark brown teddy bear from Alex's bed, and was waving it back and forth in the center of the bedroom. She was definitely trying to catch Alex's attention.

"Uh, yeah, Mom," said Alex, pulling off the headphones and looking up at her mother. She pushed her bangs out of her eyes and smiled. "What's up?"

"Don't 'yeah, Mom, what's up' me," Mrs. Mack answered. She turned to the teddy bear in her hand. "Listen, Ted," she said, addressing the bear. "Would you please tell your owner that her time is up on the laptop?"

"But, Mom," Alex moaned, looking down at the pile of papers and books around her. "I'm not done with my homework—"

"And, Ted," her mother continued, still not talking to Alex, "tell her to turn down the volume on her headphones. I can hear it all the way down the hall."

"But, Mom—"

"And, Ted, remind Alex that she's had her hour on the computer, please," said Mrs. Mack, still looking at the stuffed animal. "And the extra half hour I gave her so she could finish her homework."

"But, Mom—" Alex hesitated as Mrs. Mack held out the stuffed animal toward her daughter, indicating that she would talk only through the teddy bear. Alex rolled her eyes. She knew her mom was right about the computer, but that didn't mean she wouldn't try to make up some excuse. "All right, Ted," she answered. She was definitely glad none of her friends were around to see her talking to a bear. "Tell Mom that I was typing an e-mail to Annie and I got behind on my homework . . . and she does want Annie and me to stay in touch. She said so the other day," Alex added somewhat breathlessly as she tried to fit everything into a sentence before her mother cut her off.

"Now, Alex. You know how important this script for my drama class is, and I need to put in the finishing touches," replied Mrs. Mack, setting down the bear and standing over Alex. Mrs. Mack had been let go from her job in public relations and returned to college. One of her favorite classes so far was drama. Alex remembered that the week before, her mother's professor had announced that Mrs. Lucy Hutton, the famous English playwright, was going to critique several of the scripts, and Mrs. Mack's script was among those chosen.

Since then, Mom's been totally crazed. Make that a happy crazed, Alex thought. But that still didn't make Alex feel any better about not having the computer to finish her homework. "This wouldn't have happened if Annie hadn't taken the other computer," Alex grumbled out loud.

"I know. But you and I both know that Annie needed it for college. And we really can't afford to buy a new one right now. Besides, your father can't decide how many megabytes or gigabits—whatever they are—he can't decide how many to get. Either way, we all promised to share this laptop."

"But, Mom—"

"Hello, ladies!" said George Mack, smiling as he sailed into Alex's bedroom. "Is the computer free yet?"

Alex and her mother turned to Mr. Mack and stared.

Alex's father stopped in his tracks. "Um, bad time?" he asked, backing out into the hallway.

Mrs. Mack walked over and grabbed his arm, pulling him back into Alex's bedroom. "Gee. If looks could melt, I would be a puddle of goo right now," he added.

Alex started to laugh in spite of the computer discussion, then she bit her lip. *If only he knew that I can turn into a puddle,* she thought, *and not because someone is staring daggers at me. Not a good idea to say anything now, though.*

"Really, George," continued Mrs. Mack, shaking her head. "We really should do something about the computer situation. We all need to use it at the same time," she added, deliberately looking at Alex.

"All right, don't worry, ladies," Mr. Mack said, smiling again. "I'll just bring my laptop home from work."

"Is that the one with all of Danielle Atron's secrets on it?" asked Alex. She really didn't want to have anything to do with Danielle Atron, the president of Paradise Valley Chemical, because Alex knew that one of the company's best-kept secrets was a chemical called GC-161. She knew because she had once been doused with the chemical in an accident involving a Paradise Valley Chemical truck, and it gave her all sorts of strange powers. Now she could send electrical zappers from her fingertips and move things around the room with her telekinetic powers. The weirdest power was her ability to morph into a silvery puddle of liquid just by thinking about it.

Mr. and Mrs. Mack were wonderful parents, and Alex wasn't about to panic them by coming clean about her powers. Only the family's science whiz, Annie, who, before she went to college, loved to run experiments on Alex and Alex's best friend, Ray Alvarado, knew about her powers. And though she told them almost every other secret in the universe, Alex couldn't bring herself to tell her other two best friends, Robyn Russo and Nicole Wilson. They would definitely go ballistic.

After all, if word about Alex's powers did get out, she knew Danielle Atron, the developer of GC-161, would turn Alex into her own personal guinea pig. Ever since the accident, it seemed as if Ms. Atron was always looking for the GC-161 kid. And just for that reason, Alex was content to keep her powers a tight secret.

Mr. Mack shook his head. "No, I think I'll bring home an older model we have in the lab. We can hook it up to our printer, and it has a modem, so you can still e-mail your sister," he added. "But you'll have to wait an extra nanosecond for your messages."

Alex pretended to wince. "A whole nanosecond? Boy, Dad. You sure know how to torture a person, don't you," she said, joking.

"Now, my turn. Pack it up," said Mrs. Mack, standing by Alex and the laptop. "I have a script to work on. Broadway awaits!"

"But, Mom—" Alex started to protest again, then she stopped and brightened. She gathered her papers and books from the desk, and headed out the door. "You can have the laptop, Mom. I have an idea."

Alex flew down the stairs and pitched the papers and books onto the living room couch. She made a beeline for the kitchen and grabbed the receiver from the phone on the wall, punching in a number she knew by heart.

"Hello, Russo residence. How may I help you?" said a low, businesslike voice.

"Robyn. That you?" Alex pulled back the receiver and stared at it, then put it to her ear again.

"Oh, hi, Alex," came the normal voice of her friend. "What's up?"

"I should ask you the same," Alex replied. "What's with the funny voice and way you answered?"

"Oh, my mother keeps getting all these calls from people wanting to give money to some charity drive her club is sponsoring," Robyn said. "So she said she wants me to answer the phone more professionally and not like a crazed teenager. How did I sound?"

"Um, great, I guess. But not really like you."

"I'm not supposed to sound like me. I think I was trying to sound like Katharine Hepburn. Did you ever see her in *The African Queen* with Humphrey Bogart? I mean she was great, but all those swamps she had to go through. And the bugs. Not to mention the leeches. Gross. Can you imagine—"

"Robyn, excuse me, can I ask a question?" Alex knew if she didn't cut into Robyn's thoughts, she would never get her homework done tonight. As she started talking, she knew she was rambling, but she tried to give Robyn all the details of why she needed a computer. "So can I come over and use your computer?" Alex asked after explaining the entire story to Robyn. There was a short silence on the other end of the line. "Robyn? You still there?"

"Sure. I didn't follow you, but that's all right. Come on over anyway. Oh, and I know what I wanted to ask you," Robyn added. "Remember my aunt over on Pine Street? Well, I volunteered to walk her dog *and* her two cats while she's on vacation. Don't laugh, but my aunt thinks her cats should get the same attention as her dog. Anyway, she's leaving on Saturday morning. Wanna help?"

Alex hesitated. Robyn earned money by watching other people's pets—or at least she always seemed to get hooked into doing it. Alex didn't really like it as much as Robyn, but after all, Robyn *was* letting Alex use her computer. "All right, Robyn. I'll help."

"Great! Oh, and did I tell you that my mom's friend from England is coming here for two weeks? She has a fifteen-year-old daughter named Amy. We've written back and forth for years. I saw her a long time ago, but I can't remember what she looks like. Dark hair, I think. Kind of tall. But then again, my memory isn't what it used to be. Probably from all that stuff I've had to jam in my brain for school. Or maybe all those chemicals in the food at the cafeteria. Anyway, Mrs. Hutton and Amy should be here late tonight, and then—"

"Wait a minute. Did you say *the* Mrs. Hutton?" interrupted Alex.

"Yeah, right. Why?"

Alex was stunned. "As in Lucy Hutton?"

Robyn laughed. "Yeah. That's Amy's mother. Why? You know her?"

"Not really. I've just heard about her all week," Alex answered.

"You what?"

"Never mind, Robyn. I'll tell you all about it when I get over there," answered Alex. After she and Robyn said good-bye, Alex stuffed her papers and books in her knapsack. It was weird that her mom had just been talking about Mrs. Hutton, the playwright who was going to critique her script. Alex cringed at the thought of another foreign visitor. After all, not too long ago, a foreign exchange student from France turned out to be a spy who was trying to find the GC-161 kid. *Hopefully, this girl won't be a spy,* she thought, shivering, *or a relation to the security chief at Paradise Valley Chemical.* She shook her head, then ran up the stairs to tell her mother she was off to Robyn's house.

Dear Alex,
Don't you just love computers? I'm tutoring in computer lab right now and I'm surrounded by 30 of them! It's like being in heaven! Computers are wonderful—I don't know what I'd do if I couldn't use one! . . . Did I tell you my roommate has the flu? She's at the infimary. So I have the room to myself for a while . . . If you, Mom, and Dad are fighting over the laptop, maybe this will give them the push to buy that new one with the fastest processor yet! Then I'll give you mine—and I'll keep the new one :) . . . Yes, I'll send Ray a T-shirt—what color? . . . I got an A on that history test two days ago . . . Love, Annie P.S. The tennis racket is in the bedroom closet.

CHAPTER 2

Dear Annie,
Alex mentioned to me that your roommate had the flu. Now you know the drill—eat right and get plenty of rest (that's your mother talking!). Your father still won't budge on a new computer. Something about how it's already obsolete an hour after you buy it. My script is almost ready. I'm already nervous, and Mrs. Hutton isn't even here yet! I better get back to it. Oh, and a phone call would be nice. Love, Mom

Communications and Media was one of Alex's favorite classes. Not only did she like the teacher,

Mrs. Marvin, but she also enjoyed the fact that most of her good friends were in the class, especially Robyn, Nicole, Ray, and Louis Driscoll. It was Friday, when the class would be given their assignment for the next two weeks. Most of the homework had been fun, and the last assignment had been the best: to start a journal of current events story ideas for a newspaper. Alex managed to get one of the top marks in the class for her efforts.

Alex smiled at Mrs. Marvin as she walked into the classroom. Choosing the desk next to Robyn's, Alex dropped her dark green backpack on the floor and adjusted the blue baseball cap on her head.

Sitting behind Robyn was a girl about Alex's age. She was dressed all in black, and had short brunet hair. At the end of her long, lanky arms, she was holding the Sunday *Times* newspaper from London. "Alex, this is Amy Hutton, my friend from England," introduced Robyn. "She got in late last night after you left."

"Hi," Alex said. "Like it here?"

"So far," replied Amy, folding up the newspaper. She pushed a lock of hair behind her ear and Alex noticed three small earrings along Amy's right ear lobe. "But all I've seen today is the back of Robyn's head," she joked, poking Robyn in the back.

Robyn grimaced at the jab, then smiled back at the English girl. "Don't worry. I'll take you to a much nicer place this afternoon. Like to the mall."

"How about that art museum your mum promised?" asked Amy, leaning forward.

Before Robyn answered, Alex felt someone poke her in the back with a notebook. "Hey, Al, did you get your English paper done last night?" Alex turned to see Ray sitting behind her and Louis beside Ray.

"Yeah. Finally," she replied, zipping open her pack and pulling out her paper. She held it up so Ray could see it.

Robyn snorted. "She had to borrow my computer last night," she said, putting in a barrette to hold back a stray lock of her red hair. "Something about her mom hogging a laptop."

"So you still can't convince your dad to buy a new one, Alex?" asked Nicole, setting her books down on the desk behind Louis and sitting down. "Actually, that may be good." Alex slipped the paper back into her backpack and turned to her friend, sensing a lecture coming on. "There should be a law that you have to keep your computer for more than five years before you get a new one," continued Nicole. "Then we wouldn't be throwing so many computers away and filling up the landfills, not to mention using up all that energy to make so many of them."

"Yeah, my dad seems to buy one ever other week. I'm beginning to think his great dream is to have two computers in every room," added Dave Bullard, trying to slip into the seat in front of Alex's. Dave was one of the tallest and thinnest people Alex had ever seen, and she felt sorry for him as he tried to fit himself in at any of the school's small desks. Dave was a new student and no one knew much about him. Alex knew he liked computers, though. She often overheard Dave and Louis talking in the halls about the latest computer games they bought or downloaded from the Internet.

"Wow. Really? A computer in every room?

Talk about overload," said Amy, scrunching her nose at Dave.

"I wish my dad was like that," interjected Louis. "Then I could buy 'The Savage Trolls of Mongo.' You know, that new software that's being reviewed in all the gaming magazines. Right now, we don't have enough memory in our system to run the thing."

"Have that," interrupted Emily Baker as she sat down on the other side of Alex. Emily had long black hair pulled back in a braid, and always seemed to wear red. Alex thought it was so that anyone could spot Emily a mile away. Alex also knew better than to try to top Emily when it came to computers. She had been one of the top students in Alex's computer class last semester, and she let everyone know it. "My mother bought the game for my little brother last week," Emily continued, adjusting the red ribbon woven through her braided hair. "He could only reach level two, so he gave it to me. I'm on level five already."

Alex noticed the adoring look in Louis's eyes as he stared at Emily. "Wow. Level five? I think I'm in love."

"Don't even think it," Emily said, scowling at Louis. She spoke to Alex. "I know one thing. One day, computers will take care of everything and do everything for us. We won't have to go anywhere, just pop on some special glasses and walk through the Grand Canyon. Or hike to the top of Mount Everest."

"Yeah, and walk on Mars," added Louis, still staring at Emily.

Ray shrugged. "Oh, I don't know. I'd rather go to the Grand Canyon in person. You know, on one of those donkeys that takes you all the way to the bottom."

"I agree with Ray," added Alex. "I'd rather go in person. I don't think computers will ever be able to take the place of people. They can't think like humans, so how do you expect them to handle everything? Let's see a computer have the talent to, say, take beautiful pictures with a camera."

As Emily made a snorting noise, Mrs. Marvin opened her briefcase on the front desk. "All right, gang," Mrs. Marvin said. The room quieted down. "First, I know many of you have already met her in some of your other classes today, but I'd like you all to welcome our visitor, Amy Hutton. She's from England, and her mother is the playwright, Lucy Hutton." Everyone in the class turned to look at Amy. She put down the newspaper she had picked up again and smiled, then turned her attention to Mrs. Marvin. "Second, I was listening to your discussion just before class started. So some of you think computers are the answer to everything?" Alex noticed Louis and Emily nod vigorously. "And some of you think we need the human touch?" Alex and Ray nodded. "Maybe it's time to put your money where your mouth is."

"What money?" asked Ray. Several students chuckled.

Mrs. Marvin smiled, then continued. "I'm sure having everything done for you by computer would be a wonderful convenience," she said, walking up and down the aisles between the rows of desks. "But what if the electricity goes out?"

"And don't forget that the daft spell checker can't distinguish between homonyms like *flour* and *flower*," added Amy, raising her hand.

"Yes, thank you, Amy," answered Mrs. Marvin. "You're right. And let's not forget about the ability to use your imagination or your gut feelings." No one said a word, and several students moved uncomfortably in their seats. Mrs. Marvin walked back to the front of the class. "I've been thinking about your next assignment for quite a while, and after listening to you today, I've decided to offer you all a challenge: I want you to write at least two newsletters."

Ray smiled broadly and poked Alex in the back again. "Cool, huh?" he whispered. Alex held her finger to her lips, letting Ray know she was listening intently to their assignment. She was trying to do her best in this class so she could raise her overall average. Plus, it would feel great to get the best mark again.

"I'm going to split you into two groups with six students in each group," Mrs. Marvin continued. She held up her hand and pointed down the center of the room, then moved her hand to the right, toward Emily, Louis, and Nicole. "This side of the room will write their newsletters using the school's computers. You can do e-mail interviews, use the computers as word processors, and use any high-tech machines you want to. Emily? You seem to think computers are the only way, so you'll be in charge of this group."

Mrs. Marvin turned toward Alex's side of the room. "And for those of you on this side it will be just the opposite. I want you to use typewriters and paper and pens, cut and paste pictures, do interviews in person, and you can't use any high-tech machines. That means no computers, e-mail, or laser printers. I want it done the old fashioned way. Alex? You said you didn't think computers were the be-all and end-all, I think you'd be perfect to run this group."

Alex jumped in her seat, surprised that she was chosen to head the group. "Me?" she said, gulping.

"Perfect!" Alex heard Amy say.

Mrs. Marvin nodded. "You'll all be graded on your resourcefulness, not to mention the newsletters' design, content, and accuracy. The first one will be due next Wednesday. That gives you the weekend and two days to get it together." The entire class moaned when they heard the date. "Not only that, I want the entire school to see your newsletters, so you'll also be judged by your peers and some teachers. The best newsletter group gets the best grade."

As Mrs. Marvin got something from her briefcase, almost everyone in the class started talking about the assignment. Alex turned toward the others in her group and noticed that everyone except Amy was shocked, but no one more than Alex. She looked down and realized her hands were starting to sweat, and they hadn't even started yet.

A flash of red caught Alex's eye. Turning in her seat, she saw Emily smiling smugly at her. She tried to smile back but she knew it was only a grimace. *Is this ever going to be a long weekend or what,* Alex thought, leaning back in her seat with a sigh.

Dear Rodney and Randy: I bet you never thought you'd get an e-mail from me! But here I am, Louis the Great of Paradise Valley! How are Aunt Janet and Uncle John? . . . We have this cool project we're doing for one of my classes at school. We have to write a dazzling newsletter using the computer, while another group only gets to use an antique typewriter!

Man, are we ever going to run rings around that group! And yours truly is in charge of gathering information on the Internet. I just thought I'd sneak in a little note to you guys while I'm surfing for stories here at school . . . Did you catch the new computer game, "Taco Terror"? Check it out—it's cool! Scanners indicate a teacher is near—gotta go . . . Louis

CHAPTER 3

Hi, Annie,

Ray wants a light gray T-shirt. Thanks . . . Remember that I told you that I liked my Communications and Media class? NOT! Well, at least, not right now. We have to put together a newsletter. Some kids (Nicole and Louis are on the other team) get to use the computer, and others have to do it the old (I say slow!) way—with typewriters, paste, paper and pen, and stuff like that. Guess who was chosen to head the old group? Stop laughing, Annie. At least Robyn and Ray are on my team . . . Love, Alex P.S. No tennis racket in the bedroom closet. Any other bright ideas?

Alex stared at the laptop computer monitor on the kitchen table. She typed in a few commands, and the computer drive hummed, then displayed the message, "E-mail message transfer successful." She hit a few more keys on the keyboard and watched as the computer program shut down, then switched off the computer's power.

"All yours, Mom," she said, pushing the laptop in front of her mother.

"Thanks, dear," Mrs. Mack said, adjusting her papers on the table. She sat up straighter in the chair and turned on the computer.

Alex leaned back in her chair and looked around the kitchen. "Boy, what a mess," she muttered under her breath.

Papers were everywhere, spread out on the kitchen table, counters, and chairs. Dave Bullard had written a sports story about the Paradise High girl's basketball team and Ray had left her a note suggesting a story on the latest adventure movie playing at the local multiplex. Robyn wanted to write a story about the upcoming holiday dance. Jake Gold and Sara-Jo Roberto, the other two members of Alex's group, had handed her more ideas: Jake wanted to write a profile of the new chemistry teacher and Sara-Jo suggested a piece about her experiences in driver's education class. Alex, herself, had jotted down an outline on how to take better pictures with a camera at the prom, a sports event, or a party.

These are all great story ideas, she thought, *so why do I feel as if we're already behind?* She sighed loudly as she remembered a conversation she had had with Emily just a few hours before, and how her team already had at least six stories for their newsletter typed into the computer by the end of that Friday.

"Did you say something, Alex?" came a voice behind a newspaper. George Mack was standing at the kitchen counter, skimming through the sports section. "Hey, finally," he said, responding to something he'd read. "They're going to put in that new baseball stadium in Rutherford."

"Hmm, yes, dear. Maybe if I change this line to . . ." Mrs. Mack said, pressing several keys.

Alex looked over at her father and made a face. "You're worried about baseball stadiums while my entire academic career goes *poof,*" she said, motioning to the papers around her. "Just look at all this stuff I have to go through." She picked up Dave's paper and stared at the handwriting. "Doesn't anyone know how to write clearly anymore? Dad, can you tell what this word is? *Disgusted* or *dissected?*"

Mr. Mack leaned over and squinted at the paper. "Looks like *digested* to me. What's the context?"

" 'The Paradise High girl's basketball team digested the other team'?"

"Could be. I've heard that term in sports before. 'The Jets digested the Redskins.' Then again, maybe that's not an accurate example," he said thoughtfully, then turned back to the sports section again.

Alex looked at her mother with hope. "Can you figure out this word, Mom?"

"Only if you'll figure out if I should eliminate this line or not," she answered, still poring over the text on the computer screen.

Alex sighed deeply again. *It's times like this when I really miss Annie. She'd have some bright idea of how to sort out this mess, and she'd be able to read Dave's writing, I bet,* Alex thought. "What I really need right now," she said out loud, looking wistfully at the laptop sitting in front of her mother, "is a typewriter."

"Wait a minute," said Mr. Mack, folding the newspaper and tucking it under his arm. "You mean I brought home that extra laptop so you and your mom wouldn't— Oh, that's right." He hesitated as he noticed the piles of paper around the room. "You can't use the computer."

"Well, I'm finished for the night. I'm beat," said Alex, stacking the papers together. She grabbed the pile, stood up slowly, and walked out of the kitchen, dragging her feet. Mr. Mack shook his head and looked at Mrs. Mack. "Computer withdrawal, if you ask me," he said.

Alex didn't feel much better when she woke up on Saturday. All night long she had had dreams about printing—and reprinting—the newsletters by hand. Then she overslept. Then the old jeans she wanted to wear to help Robyn walk the animals were in the wash. To top everything off, her favorite cereal was almost gone, only crumbs remained. And all she could do when she met Robyn and Amy was complain about the newsletter.

"Don't worry, Alex. It'll work out," said Amy, trying to balance the *Times of London* and Willie, the Persian cat, in her arms.

"Yeah, Alex. We'll figure something out," Robyn was saying, as she tried to hook a leash to the white Angora cat's flea collar. "Come on, Artie, hold still," she muttered to the cat.

"Right. Keep telling me." As Alex leaned down and rubbed Buster behind the ears, the big brown dog chewed at his leash. It was a windy and warm day, perfect for walking the animals. She pulled Buster along—or Buster pulled her—and they approached Robyn's house. "But every time I passed Emily in the hall yesterday, she had this smug smile on her face."

"Emily will never win a congeniality contest," Robyn added, watching as Artie stopped and rolled over on his back. The cat purred as Robyn tugged at his leash.

Alex nodded. "That's for sure. I wish we could use a computer for just a few things. You know, maybe just the front page, or maybe just the photo captions—"

"Really, Alex, you don't need those things, remember?" said Amy, shaking her head. She shifted the cat and the newspaper again.

"I know, Amy, but things are so much easier when you do use computers. I guess I just miss it— Hey, there's your mom, Robyn," Alex added, waving to the woman digging around several colorful flowers in the Russos' garden. Mrs. Russo smiled and waved her straw hat at them, then turned back to her plants.

Buster barked furiously at Mrs. Russo's hat and pulled at his leash. Suddenly Alex felt as if her arm were being pulled from its socket as Buster headed right toward the open garden gate with Alex in tow. Alex was trying to hold on and pull Buster back, but the big dog was too strong. She cringed as she heard a *snap!* The leash had broken.

Out of the corner of her eye, Alex saw Willie squirm away from Amy and Artie pull his leash away from Robyn. Both cats were trying to catch up with Buster, all the animals heading toward the open gate. Robyn and Amy both let out a yell and raced past Alex to catch up with the animals.

But Alex held back. She noticed that Mrs.

Russo still had her back turned, oblivious to what was happening, and Robyn and Amy were far ahead. She just had to take the chance. As a gust of wind blew, she concentrated hard, telekinetically swinging the gate shut. But she was too late. Buster pushed his snout inside, slipping in just before the gate closed.

The two cats stopped cold and Robyn scooped them up in her arms. Reaching Amy's side, Alex breathed a sigh of relief. "Thank goodness for the wind," said Robyn.

But Alex's relief didn't last long. Looking over the gate and into the garden, she saw Mrs. Russo. The woman was covered with mud, her hat cocked to one side of her head, and she was holding Buster by his collar. Yellow, red, and orange flowers surrounded Robyn's mother as if a hurricane had suddenly hit all the flower beds. "Guess what you three will be doing this afternoon," said Mrs. Russo.

Alex, Robyn, and Amy gulped.

"Certainly won't be having an audience with the Queen," said Amy, whispering.

Alex nodded. She knew that she, Robyn, and Amy would spend the rest of the afternoon repairing the damage to Mrs. Russo's garden, putting each plant back into its proper place. Alex's first full day to work on the newsletter was definitely shot. Now she'd really be behind.

Hi, Alex,
Tell Mom and Dad I'll try to give them a call tomorrow—I'm going to a basketball game this afternoon, then a bunch of us are going to the movies, that new techno-movie I told you about the other night—the one with all the neat computer graphics . . . I'll send Ray his T-shirt Monday. Oh, and tell Mom that I haven't received the Girl Scout cookie box yet (she promised a week ago!). Tell her it's the only way to keep away the flu bug that's going around. :) . . . Good luck with the newsletter. Love, Annie P.S. The racket's in the downstairs closet.

CHAPTER 4

Dear Kathy:
Thanks for your note. I agree entirely with your idea. I think we should look for an alternative to the fuels that produce our electricity. Maybe more solar power. But right now, I guess I have to be careful of what I hope for—I need the electricity right now! In one of my classes, I have to help put together several newsletters using everything that uses electricity—computers, printers, scanners, the Internet. At least I've tried to do my part by insisting that they print the newsletter on recycled paper! Our group seems to be winning

already. We're almost done with our first newsletter—long before the other group. The only thing I don't like is that too many of my friends are in the other group—and our group leader is, shall we say, a bit aggressive. Hope to hear from you soon. Nicole

It was the middle of the morning on Sunday, and Alex, Ray, Robyn, and Amy sat on the front lawn of the Macks' house. Alex rolled up the sleeves of her yellow T-shirt, feeling the warmth of the sun on her aching arms. Yesterday she, Robyn, and Amy had spent most of the afternoon replanting Mrs. Russo's garden, and Alex's muscles felt as if she had planted all the flowers in Paradise Valley. Then this morning, she helped her mom and dad with the house cleaning. *Another reason why I miss Annie,* she thought, closing her eyes. *She used to help with the cleaning. Now I have to do her part, too.*

While Alex and Ray discussed their lack of a typewriter, Robyn and Amy read through the *Times*. Amy was wearing all black again, with clunky black shoes. Alex wondered if Amy was too hot wearing black and sitting in the sun.

"So I asked Mr. Hess, and he said the only typewriters they had at the school were being used in the office," said Ray, picking at a blade of grass. "Then my dad suggested I call an electronics store. But I can guarantee none of us have that kind of spare cash sitting around."

"So now what?" asked Alex, lying back on the grass.

Ray shrugged and looked over at Amy. "Do you always carry around a newspaper?"

"Of course. Mr. Russo picks it up for me at the bookstore," Amy said, leaning over the newspaper. "I love newspapers. I collect them wherever I go. And the British ones keep me up to date on what's going on back home. You know, like the review of my mum's latest play and the report on the Oasis concert," she added, pointing to an article in the paper and smiling.

"Cool!" Ray said, moving closer to the paper.

Alex turned as the front door opened and her mother shook out a rug. "Well, isn't this a cheery group," said Mrs. Mack, throwing the rug across her arm. "Alex, your dad and I were just thinking about the typewriter you need. What about a consignment shop? There are a bunch not too far from here." Mrs. Mack stared as Alex, Ray, and Robyn heaved a collective sigh.

"Right," replied Ray. "Even if we did find one, I bet we don't have a dollar between us. I just spent all my money taking Mary out the other night. We went to see *Harmless and Clueless.*"

"What?" exclaimed Alex and Robyn in unison.

"You took her to *that* movie? On a first date?" asked Robyn.

"I liked that movie," said Amy. Ray smiled in her direction.

"Well, anyway, if anyone is interested," said Mrs. Mack, emphasizing the last word, "I have to go to the grocery store. While I shop, you can look for a typewriter."

"Money, Mom?" Alex asked, resting her head in her hand.

"I'll help if it's not too expensive," she replied. Alex noticed that her mother was in a super-generous mood. It must have been because Amy's mother was going to hear the drama class scripts, and as Alex's mom said, finally a real professional would judge her work. *Maybe it's time to ask for that new computer,* she thought. *Naw. I can't use it for the newsletter anyway.*

Alex sighed as they entered the last shop on the street. They had already tried three other stores, but with no luck. Two of the owners just laughed when Alex asked if they had any typewriters. The other owner asked Alex if she was on a treasure hunt—after all, no one uses a typewriter any more.

The last antique shop on the street was also where Alex and the others were to meet Mrs. Mack. As Alex looked over at the dingy windows, she put her hand on the doorknob and hesitated. "Oh, go ahead," encouraged Ray. "We'll be right behind you if anyone tries to put you on a shelf and sell you."

Alex scowled at Ray, then turned the knob and walked in. She shivered as she scanned the cold, damp room. The inside of the shop was small and drab, with cobwebs in the upper corners of the room. It almost looked like a haunted house she had gone to one Halloween.

Robyn moved closer to Alex. "This is definitely creepy, Alex," she said, sniffing the air.

"It smells like old, musty furniture. Old *creepy*, musty furniture."

"Yeah," whispered Ray, his eyes opening wide. "And the furniture probably came from all the haunted houses in Paradise Valley."

Alex and Robyn's heads swiveled quickly toward Ray. "Ray," whispered Alex, "you and your ghost stories."

As Ray chuckled, Amy leaned closer to Alex and Robyn. "No, he may be right," she said in a low, soft voice, looking around her. "We have plenty of ghosts in England. You probably have them here, too. And they usually hang out in grotty places like this."

Alex, Robyn, and Ray were no longer smiling. They all shivered as they stared at Amy.

"Ahem!" came a voice behind them.

Alex jumped and noticed that the other three jumped, too. As she turned to the voice, something caught her eye: two old typewriters, an electric and a manual, sitting near a short, balding man at the counter.

Ray leaned closer to Alex and whispered in her ear. "Wow. Is he a dead ringer for Vince or what?" Alex shivered again at the reference to the chemical plant. Vince once worked as head of security for Paradise Valley Chemical and was always in search of the GC-161 kid—in other words, for Alex. She had to admit the man did look like Vince, but it may have been the nasty scowl on his face that gave him the same sinister expression.

"What do you kids want?" the man behind the counter asked, putting down a silver bowl he was cleaning. He looked over his glasses. "The lot of you are always trying to sell things to me," he grumbled. "Candy bars. Magazine subscriptions. Smelly soap. You aren't selling anything, are you?"

Alex gulped. "No, sir. We were just looking for a—well—typewriters," she answered, pointing to the two machines.

The man looked at the typewriters, then at Alex. He eyed her suspiciously. "What do you kids want with a typewriter? Seems to me you all have enough fancy computers to do your work for you now, eh?"

"It's a special project," Ray explained. "We're trying to write a newsletter, but we can't use computers."

"Nice story, young man," the man said, picking up the bowl again. "But I don't buy it. And anyway, I know you kids can't afford a typewriter. So just go back to selling whatever and let me do my work here."

"How much are the typewriters," asked Robyn. When the man looked over his glasses at her and sneered, she moved behind Alex. "Just curious," she muttered.

"The manual is forty dollars and the electric is sixty dollars," said the man, continuing to polish the bowl.

As Alex shook her head, she heard an *oops!* behind her. Turning, she noticed Amy had walked into a shelf and it was now tilting to the left. Reaching out with her left hand, Alex grabbed the shelf. She held her breath as the shelf's contents—several glass and ceramic jars—stabilized.

"Clumsy of me," said Amy, staring at Alex. "Can't thank you enough, Alex. I didn't even see—"

"That's it!" thundered the man from behind the counter. "I don't need you kids badgering me about typewriters and then knocking down all my antiques." He put down the bowl again and pointed to the door. "Now, out!"

As Alex and the others pushed their way toward the front of the store, the bell on the door tinkled and in walked Mrs. Mack. Amazingly, as Alex and the others watched, the shopkeeper seemed to change into another person right before their eyes. Stepping from behind the counter, he straightened his tie, smiled broadly, and reached out to take Mrs. Mack's hand. "Mrs. Mack," he said, his voice seeming to ooze goodness.

"Now I know this place is haunted," whispered Ray to Alex. "First by Mr. Hyde, then by Dr. Jekyll," he said. Alex nodded, remembering the Robert Louis Stevenson book, *Dr. Jekyll and Mr. Hyde* from English class. The man did seem to change from nasty to wonderful in a heartbeat.

Mrs. Mack took the man's hand and shook it. "Mr. Teeter! How are you? Oh, I see you've met my daughter and her friends?"

"This is your daughter?" he asked, smiling. He walked over to Robyn and put his arm around her shoulders. "What a lovely girl."

"Uh, no, Mr. Teeter. The girl in the yellow T-shirt," corrected Mrs. Mack, pointing at Alex.

"Ah, yes," he said, extending his hand to Alex. "It's a shame I never had you in class. Now I did have your sister. And she was—well, one of the best. I can remember the time when she aced one of my most difficult pop quizzes. Something to do with square roots of imaginary numbers." Mr. Teeter seemed to glow with pride.

Mrs. Mack noticed the stunned look on Alex's face. "This is Mr. Teeter, Alex. Annie's math teacher from two years ago. Remember? Annie used to talk about him all the time," said her mother, emphasizing the last few words. Alex, still stunned, nodded as she shook Mr. Teeter's hand. "He's retired from teaching and opened his own store, right?" Mrs. Mack continued. Mr. Teeter nodded. "These are Alex's friends, Robyn, Ray, and Amy. They're looking for a typewriter, Mr. Teeter. They have a school project to do, and they can't use a computer. What about those?" she asked, pointing to the two typewriters on the counter.

"We were just talking about them, weren't we, kids?" He smiled in Robyn's direction, then turned back to Mrs. Mack. As Ray started to contradict Mr. Teeter, Alex put a hand on his arm, silently warning him not to say anything—at least not until they got the typewriters. "Well, they *have* been sitting there for about a year."

"Actually, Mr. Teeter, they won't need them for very long. Just a few weeks," added Mrs. Mack. Alex noticed she was giving one of her prize-winning smiles to Mr. Teeter.

"Hmmm. Well, in that case, how about if I lease them to you, for, say, twenty dollars for two weeks? Will that be long enough?"

Alex looked at her mother. "Mom, we could wash the car a few times, do the lawn—"

"Don't worry, Alex," she said, smiling and pulling a twenty-dollar bill from her purse. "We can talk about that later. Mr. Teeter, you have a deal."

Mr. Teeter walked behind the counter again and put the cash in the register. "Thank you so much, Mrs. Mack. I'm sure these wonderful kids will take good care of the typewriters. Any sister of Annie's is all right in my book," he said, hugging Robyn again. Robyn forced a smile, realizing Mr. Teeter still thought she was Alex. Ray and Alex each picked up a typewriter. "And good luck with your project, kids," he added happily as they murmured their thanks.

"I think I liked Mr. Hyde better," Ray whispered to Alex as they walked out the door.

Dear Annie: How is school going? Love, Dad

CHAPTER 5

Dear Annie,
I'm beat. We almost finished the first newsletter tonight. Just a few more pages. So I think we'll make the deadline. There's even a story on the origin of our school mascot. (Did you know we were originally supposed to be the Paradise Penguins???) . . . The girl from England, Amy Hutton, is here with her mom and she's staying with Robyn. She seems nice. I took her to see your "science setup" in the garage and she banged into that weird glass thing on the left side of your desk. I caught it before it crashed to the ground. And chill,

Annie. I didn't even use you-know-what to catch it. . . . On Wednesday night, Ray, Robyn, Amy, and I are doing something that's right up your alley: We're going to the local observatory for a story. Ray's interviewing the guy (sorry, astronomer) who runs the place—while Robyn and Amy help me take photos (that part I really like). I hope I can take a picture of that new comet. Wouldn't that be cool! . . . Love, Alex . . . P.S. I've given up on the tennis racket. We probably gave it away.

Alex was exhausted. It was Monday and she was trying to stay awake toward the end of homeroom. She knew why she was so tired: Late yesterday afternoon, Alex and the others in her group gathered again at the Mack house to type the stories for the first newsletter. Mr. Mack went out and bought several pizzas. In between munching slices, Alex and Dave typed the articles. Ray, Robyn, Sara-Jo, and Jake checked spelling and grammar using the numerous dictionaries, thesauruses, and reference books piled high on the kitchen table. Amy was out with her mother visiting Mrs. Hutton's friends in the theater, but she said she'd like to help next time. *We sure could have used an extra pair of hands last night,* Alex thought, sighing. *Or maybe I should have just used my powers.*

By the time they finished, three hours later, they had just barely typed in the first four pages of the newsletter. There were several more pages left to type and seven photos left to cut and paste inside the newsletter.

As Alex dragged herself to her first class, Nicole came running up. "Alex, now don't get mad. I didn't really have anything to do with it, honest," Nicole said, holding up her hand. "I didn't even know—"

Just as suddenly, Robyn, Amy, and Ray came running up. Ray was waving a paper in his hand. "You're not going to believe this, Al," he said, somewhat breathlessly, interrupting Nicole. "It's the other group's newsletter. It's out two days early and they say they're going to put one out every other day." Alex groaned and leaned against a nearby locker. "And that's not all," Ray added, looking over at Nicole, then at Alex. "Look at the headline."

"That's what I was trying to warn you about," added Nicole.

Alex was suddenly wide awake. She looked at the paper and blinked her eyes, then blinked them again. The words were still there: "Mack Smacks Garden!" As she skimmed the story, she realized what it was all about. The article told how Alex lost control of the dog that wrecked Mrs. Russo's flower garden. And it implied that Alex had let the dog go on purpose.

Alex was fuming. As she finished the article, she saw the author's name at the bottom of the page. It was written by Emily Baker, with quotes from an anonymous source.

"Now calm down, Alex," said Nicole. "At least I didn't write it—or Louis. And neither one of us knew that Emily had put it in. She must have done it at the last minute. You can do that with computers. Really."

Alex looked at her friend and nodded. "I believe you, Nicole. Really."

"Great. Gotta go, Alex," Nicole said, patting Alex on the shoulder and slipping into the crowd walking down the hallway.

Alex sighed. "It's not that Emily wrote about

me, but that the story is all wrong," she said to the others, slapping the paper with her hand. "I didn't wreck the garden on purpose, and she didn't even mention that we fixed it up afterward. How could Emily print such garbage? And who's this anonymous source?"

"That would be me," said Amy, letting her voice trail off and fussing with the copy of the *Times* in her hand.

Alex and Robyn turned to the English girl. "You?" they asked in unison.

"I thought it was funny, so I just told Emily about it," answered Amy. "And I never said you did it on purpose."

"Oh, it's not your fault, Amy," said Alex, quickly glancing at the rest of the newsletter. "I guess I'm just mad because Emily made me sound like a dufus. And I'm mad because we can't put our newsletter together this fast—" Alex hesitated. "Hey, look, this says the girl's basketball team was playing the Wasps. It was the Hornets!"

"Seen one bug, you've seen them all," said Ray.

Alex scowled at him. "That's not the point,"

she said, skimming the back page. "There are mistakes all through this thing. Here's another one. The school doesn't run parallel to Bickworth Avenue, it's parallel to Beckwith Avenue."

"So our newsletter will be better, right?" asked Robyn hopefully.

"If it ever gets out," Alex said, still scanning the newsletter. She looked up when there was no response. Her friends were looking terribly uncomfortable. *Come on, Alex,* she thought. *You are the group's leader. Time to rally the troops.* She took a deep breath. "You bet we'll have a better paper, guys," she said out loud. "We won't let this get in our way. In fact—" Alex froze as she looked down the hall and saw someone in red standing with Louis near an open classroom door. They were staring in Alex's direction.

It was Emily, with the same smirk on her face. As Louis smiled and waved to Alex, Emily held up her newsletter. "The next one's coming out soon, Mack," she called to Alex. "How about yours?" She turned back to Louis and chuckled.

Ray started to move toward Louis, but Alex held his arm. "Chill, Ray. I'm not too happy about Louis being in on this, either. But remember how driven he was when he wrote for our junior high school paper, the *Atomizer?*"

"Do I ever," answered Ray, still fuming. "But I thought he learned his lesson."

Alex didn't answer. She folded up the newsletter and stuffed it into her backpack. "Come on. Let's get to class."

Dear Theresa:
You would not believe this place! There are computers everywhere! You would be in heaven. And these technoids don't even know how good they have it. I wish I could make them understand that having a computer is nice, but so is doing things our way. How is Maurice doing with the paste-up of the newspaper? I told him to ask you questions if something came up. Anyway, since you're just about the only one in the world I know who owns a computer, I decided to e-mail you. I'll check for your answer later this week. Yours, Amy H.

CHAPTER 6

Dear Annie,

Your sister is working hard (she's in the kitchen now with her friends, putting together their newsletter). And now your mother has the luxury of working on the laptop whenever she feels like it! Speaking of school (weren't we?), did I tell you I just love my drama class! Lucy Hutton, the famous playwright, is in town, and I get to read my play in front of her! I can't wait! You never know. Maybe your mother will be a famous playwright some day! And tell me you haven't caught the flu, right? Time to do some homework. You, too! Love, Mom

"All right, Ray, you first." Alex leaned back in the kitchen chair and nodded to her friend. Thunder rumbled in the distance, and Alex could hear the rain hitting the kitchen windows.

"Ahem." Ray cleared his throat. "Notice I have my official reporter's notebook," he said, holding up a blue spiral notebook. The others in the room muttered or sighed. "Well, anyway, Dave and I went to the library after school today to seek out some more information about the mascot of Paradise High, and there it was, an entire book on the subject. In fact, we tried to stay longer, to search for more information, but the librarian kicked us out. How were we supposed to know it closed at five? Anyway, we were able to gather a little background." Ray held up about ten pages from his notebook.

"Ray, that's a little background?" Alex asked, squinting at the notebook pages.

"Yeah. I figured it's about two columns long," he said, looking over at Dave. His friend nodded in reply.

"Where are we supposed to put all that?" asked Sara-Jo, standing up and shuffling through the pages on the kitchen table. "Page six?"

"Not there. It's supposed to go on page five, remember?" said Dave, standing up, his long arm pointing to a pile of papers on the table. "I already typed up the list of contents."

Robyn rolled her eyes, then turned to Dave. "And I think it should go on page six. I think my story on toxic—"

"So where will the story on the baseball team go?" asked Jake, reaching past Robyn and pointing to the extra article on the table. Suddenly hands and arms were everywhere as they each reached for a different page and tried to talk over everyone else in the process.

"Guys," started Alex. No one paid attention to her. "Ummm. Guys—" Still the others kept talking, their voices becoming louder.

Wheeeeeeeeeet!

Everyone stopped suddenly, turning to see who was making the noise. Mrs. Mack stood at the doorway of the kitchen, her fingers still in her mouth from whistling.

"Ummm. Sorry, Mom," Alex said, standing up and apologizing. "I guess we were getting carried away, huh?"

"Slightly," she said, folding her arms. "It's

late, kids. And we're going to bed now. Between you and the thunderstorm—" Mrs. Mack shook her head.

"Gotcha, Mom," Alex said, nodding her head. "We'll be quieter, right? And not too much longer," she said, appealing to the others. Everyone nodded silently. Mrs. Mack walked back out through the kitchen door and into the living room.

Alex turned to the others. She was getting frustrated, too. Here it was the night before the first newsletter was due, and they still hadn't agreed on where certain articles would go. Not only that, Alex knew that they all felt pressured by the other group. After all, they had their first newsletter out already, and Emily had rubbed it in that another one would be out soon. *I wish Emily wasn't so smug about the whole thing,* thought Alex, *then maybe I'd—*

"I don't know about you, Alex," said Robyn, breaking into Alex's thoughts, "but I'm beginning to think the paste's getting to me. Smelling it all the time has probably killed every single smartness cell in my brain."

"What br—" Ray started to say. Alex cut him short with a look.

"Well, if you ask me, I think you're all being a bit daft," said Amy, suddenly standing up near the table. "And all this argy-bargy."

"Argy-bargy?" asked Robyn. She rested her head on her chin. "Sometimes talking with you, Amy, is like talking to a person from another country."

Amy stared at Robyn, not really knowing if she was kidding or not. "Here, bung the newsletter over and let me have a go at it," she said, reaching for the papers in front of Alex. Everyone looked perplexed. "You know, pitch it. Ummm. Throw it over," Amy continued, rolling up the sleeves of her black blouse. She looked over the typed articles and photos, alternately nodding and frowning. "Looks great so far to me. You've all done a fine job. Just put in the mascot article here." She put the papers in front of Alex and pointed to the top few pages. "And the sports story here. Type up those other stories . . . a few photos on this page . . . and Bob's your uncle."

"Who?" asked Jake. "I don't have an uncle."

"I know that one," said Robyn. "She means that's all we have to do.'"

"Right," said Amy, smiling again. "So what's the problem?"

"The lack of computers, that's the problem," moaned Dave. Sara-Jo nodded vigorously.

"You just don't know how lucky you are," said Amy, folding her arms across her chest. "Where I live, we don't have too many computers, and the ones we do have aren't all connected to the Internet. In fact, I only have one friend who has e-mail at her home."

"Aw, come on," said Ray, tapping his pencil on the table. "Every computer is attached to the Internet."

"You Americans sure take things for granted," she replied, shaking her head. "At my school, we emphasize the basics of knowledge. Many of my classes are in the arts and sciences. I know three languages, and now I'm learning Latin. My town is very well known for its Shakespearean plays, especially the ones my mother puts on. Last year, I played Puck in *A Midsummer Night's Dream*." She looked around the room at the staring faces. "You have read *A Midsummer Night's Dream,* haven't you?"

"Isn't that the one where the guy falls asleep for twenty years?" asked Ray, beaming broadly.

Alex gently slapped her friend in the arm. "Yeah, Amy. We know that one. We had to read three Shakespeare plays last year in English and that was one of them." She tilted her head. "So does all this mean that you don't know anything about computers?"

Amy chuckled. "Oh, yes. We still have to know how to use the computer, but mostly we understand that it's just a tool. There are about five computers at my school, and they're for computer class only. So when our school newspaper is put together, it's done, well, what you would call, the old-fashioned way. So I don't know what you're all squealing about. By doing it slower, and checking all the information and facts, you put out a better newsletter. Not like the other group. Here, let me help."

Amy helped Sara-Jo pull out the best text and moved photos around. She showed Robyn and Ray the best way to align the pictures and worked with Alex and Dave to line up the text better. After an hour, there were only two articles left to arrange and two photos to paste onto the last pages.

"I'm beat," said Robyn, plopping down in a nearby chair. "And I can't believe we're almost done. Nice job, Amy."

Ray nodded. "Yeah, Amy. You made that seem easy."

Alex put her arm around Amy's shoulder. "I think we owe this girl a debt of gratitude. How about putting her on the masthead?"

As the others agreed, Amy raised her hand. "No, thanks anyway. I just wanted to help. It's my mum's way. She's always wanting to help everyone. Teach the lessons of life. I guess it rubbed off on me."

"Well, it's getting late. I guess we'd better go," said Robyn. She lifted her jacket from the back of the kitchen chair and threw it over her shoulder. She turned to Alex. "Can you handle the last two pages?"

"I'll do them tonight before I go to bed," said Alex, stifling a yawn. She leaned on the table. "Or maybe tomorrow morning."

Everyone murmured good night. Alex

watched as they walked out the back door and into the night. The thunderstorm had stopped, and it was just drizzling now. She didn't know what time it was, but she knew it was late. Sighing, she looked at the mess on the kitchen table. "Gee, I sure wish Annie were here," she said quietly to the empty room. "She's good at putting together stuff like this, she and her brainy mind. I just hope she—hey, wait a minute."

Alex smiled as she looked at the photos and papers in front of her. She looked both ways, then checked for noise at the door leading from the kitchen to the living room. When she heard no one, she tiptoed back over to the papers and photos.

Concentrating hard, she used her telekinetic powers to put together the pages of the newspaper. Photos flew to the right spots on the newsletter, while the written text was lined up and pasted on the paper. In a few short minutes, Alex stood back and looked at her handiwork. "Not bad," she whispered, giving a soft whistle. "Looks like a professional job to me, Alex, old girl. Knew you could do it."

As she concentrated again, books flew across

the room to the kitchen counter and were neatly stacked. She turned back to the table, and papers glided on top of one another in another neat stack—

The kitchen door creaked behind her!

Alex turned around slowly, expecting to see her mother or father. But there stood Amy, her newspaper tucked under her arm. She was staring at Alex.

"Er, forgot my brolly," Amy said, smiling and holding up an umbrella. Amy looked around at the stacks of books and papers, then peered over Alex's shoulder, looking at the finished newsletter. "I knew you'd get it done. Smashing, just smashing," she said, still smiling, then turned to walk away.

Alex stammered. "Umm. Brolly. Smashing, right. See ya, Amy."

Alex watched Amy walk back out the door. She stood there for a while, not knowing what to do. Had Amy seen her sorting the papers and books with her powers? And there wasn't any way for her to ask Amy if she did see her using her powers. Questions like that would definitely give it away. *Great*, she thought, *I can see Emily's interview of Amy in the next newsletter. "Mack has Secret Powers."*

She picked up the newsletter pile, placed it in a box, then headed for her room. *Maybe* she'd get some sleep tonight.

Hi, Ralph!
I think you finally got that move down. But now you have to work on getting the basketball to do what I call, "Come home to Papa." You sort of throw it out, then spin it quick, and it bounces back to you. The best time to do it is right in front of your opponent! Like when you're near the basket! I'll teach you when I see you next time. . . . Gotta go. I'm working on my next story for the newsletter. I'll let you know when I get the prize for the best article! . . . Stay cool. . . . Ray

CHAPTER 7

Dear Annie,
You there? I'm still beat. And all I do is dream about typewriters. . . . I'm thinking I should just go out and buy a new tennis racket. I'll need it for gym class this semester anyway. Maybe I can rent one when I turn in our stupid typewriters. I'll keep looking . . . Love, Alex

"Alex. Just the person I wanted to see," said Mrs. Marvin, setting down her pen as she looked up. "Is that the newsletter?"

Alex nodded and stepped into the classroom. "Yes, we finished it last night. I just came by for the passes to the printers. I need one for Ray and me."

Alex was between periods. She had rushed straight from her class to her locker and then to Mrs. Marvin's room. Jake Gold's mother, the owner of a printing press, volunteered to print the group's newsletter if they brought it to her before noon. Jake had a test, but Alex and Ray had study hall during third period, a little over a half hour before noon, so it worked out perfectly. Even if they were a little late coming back, they would only miss some of their lunch period.

The printer was only two blocks from Paradise High, and besides getting the newsletter printed out, Alex thought it would be cool to see how a real printing press worked. Of course, as she explained to the others in the group, it was a perfect opportunity for another newsletter story.

"You bet. Walking in the sunshine is better than being in a classroom any day, huh?" said Mrs. Marvin, writing up the passes. "By the way, Alex. I also have a little more incentive for your group and the other group." She handed the passes to Alex. "I talked with the principal and he said he'd be glad to provide certificates for the Virtual Reality Center to the winning group."

Alex beamed. "That would be cool, Mrs. Marvin!" She hesitated as she took the passes from the teacher. "But I don't know if my group really has a chance. Working with computers is much faster. And the other team has a newsletter out. We're already behind."

"And didn't I tell you that you would be judged on all the newsletters, and by everyone in the school?" Mrs. Marvin asked. "I think you should remember the speech that got you into this assignment. Computers aren't everything. Remember how you said we still needed the human touch?"

Alex smiled and nodded. "I guess I just need a pep talk once and a while."

"You've come to the right place," said Mrs. Marvin, standing up and walking with Alex to the door. "Now get going," she added, smiling. "You have a newsletter to get printed, don't you?"

Alex knew what Mrs. Marvin meant: it sure was nice to get away from school and walk out in the warm sunshine. As she waited for Ray, she took off her jacket and wrapped it around her waist. Straightening her red baseball cap, she turned to see Ray jogging toward the door. "Hi, Ray. You said Jake said that his mom would meet us at the door?" she asked, picking up the box containing the newsletter and walking outside.

"Yeah. In the lobby at the printers." Ray had, as usual when he was outside, brought his basketball from his locker. As they walked down the steps and along the school sidewalk, he dribbled the ball, trying a few air-shots over Alex's head.

"Ray, do you know what Mrs. Marvin told me? She's giving certificates to the Virtual Reality Center to the winning newsletter team."

"Way cool! You mean if we—"

"Alex! Alex!" a voice called from the front entrance of the school. Alex turned and shielded her eyes from the sun. Robyn and Amy were standing in the doorway, motioning to Alex.

"Ray, wait," she said, stuffing the box into his hand. "Here, hold this. I'll go see what she wants." Alex ran back toward the entrance and up the stairs.

"Glad I caught you," said Robyn, her long flowered dress waving in the breeze. She shifted the books from her right arm to her left as Alex reached the steps. Amy had on a black blouse and short skirt and held her usual newspaper under her arm. "I have a test in Spanish today and I think Amy would think it's a bore. How about taking her with you to the printer's? She doesn't need a pass."

"Sure," said Alex, smiling. "After all, you helped with the newsletter."

"Quite right," answered Amy, waving goodbye to Robyn.

Covering the two blocks didn't take long. As they walked along, Alex told Ray and Amy the details about Mrs. Marvin's new offer. Then Ray gave a blow-by-blow description of his potential interview with a Mr. Gibson, who had invented a new chemical. Alex was half listening, thinking about her next story. *Maybe I should cover my sister at college,* she thought. *No, maybe something about Paradise Valley Chemical—Definitely not. Maybe . . .*

"Earth to Alex." Alex shook her head as Ray's voice cut into her thoughts. "We're here."

The printer's shop was sandwiched between a

florist and an insurance office. As Ray reached for the front door, a short, stout woman with black hair pushed it open. "Ray! Good to see you!" she said in a booming voice.

"Hey, Mrs. Gold," responded Ray, tossing the basketball in her direction. She caught it, pitched it left and right with a fake, then tossed it back to Ray.

Mrs. Gold laughed. "Still can fake you out with that move, eh, Ray?"

"Yeah, always could." Ray stood back and pointed to Alex and Amy. "This is Alex Mack, the head of our group."

"Ah, the young lady I talked with on the phone, yes?" Alex nodded and shook her hand.

"And this is Amy Hutton. She's from England," he said, continuing the introductions.

Amy nodded, then looked around, picking up a newspaper from a table. "Can I have this?" she asked Mrs. Gold. "I just love newspapers."

"Why sure, honey. Be my guest," she said, laughing, then turned to Alex. "Listen, you kids are right on time. We had an emergency printing this morning. Mike is still working on it, but he's almost finished. Is that the newsletter?" she asked, pointing to the box in Alex's hand. Mrs. Gold was so overwhelming, Alex almost forgot why she was there. Confused for a moment, she shook her head, then nodded quickly, handing the box over to Jake's mother. "Great," Mrs. Gold said, opening the box and looking at the top page. "This looks great. Can't wait to read it. I'll be right back." She closed the box and walked through a door at the back of the room.

"Ray, you never told me you knew Mrs. Gold," said Alex, whispering to her friend.

"Yeah, Jake's brother is on the basketball team," answered Ray, whispering back. "Mrs. Gold comes to all the games to cheer us on. And I mean cheer."

Suddenly the door burst open and Mrs. Gold beamed at them. "Mike is on your newsletter now. Want to see how it's printed?"

This is what Alex was waiting for, another story for the newsletter and Emily nowhere in sight.

They all walked down a short hall, then through two double doors. Alex was overwhelmed by the noise as the doors swung open. She covered her ears as she walked into the press room. "Those rollers in the back are an older method of printing," Mrs. Gold shouted above the noise, pointing to several rollers in the back of the room. "But for your newsletter, we're going to use a method called gravure printing," Mrs. Gold yelled. Not surprisingly, Alex could hear her above the noise, even with her ears covered. *That's probably why she has such a booming voice,* she thought. *She has to be heard when all the presses are going.*

"Gravure printing takes your pages and scans them with a device that is similar to the kind used for offset plates. The scanner sends the information to the computer over there," she said, pointing to a computer. Alex noticed it looked a great deal like the larger computers at school. "From there, the computer sends the signals to a machine that has diamond-pointed cutting tools called styluses. The styluses cut thousands of little pits into the copper covering of a cylinder."

Alex unblocked her ears and pulled out a notebook and pencil. She scribbled into her notebook, taking down the information as Mrs. Gold spoke. "What happens then?" she yelled, trying to make her voice heard above the sound of the press.

"Then the fun begins," Mrs. Gold continued. "That's when Mike and Joe over there start printing out your newsletter." She pointed to two men standing near the press. Both men wore dark blue overalls and black caps that read, Gold Printing. Mike, the foreman, was tall and muscular, with short dark hair. Joe, his assistant, was much shorter, with long sandy hair tied back in a ponytail. "The deeper pits carry the most ink and print the darker tones, the shallower pits carry less ink, and they print the lighter tones. See?" she said, motioning to a batch of paper coming out of the printer.

"Cool!" Ray yelled, turning to see the newsletter popping out. Alex watched with pride as the newsletter skimmed past them on the printing rolls. She squinted and just caught the headline of the newsletter as it ran past her. WELCOME TO THE PH TIMES!—the name they had all chosen for the newsletter. Below the headline was the editorial she had written to explain the newsletter contest, complete with a photo of her taken by Robyn. *Let's see Emily top this one,* she thought, smiling contentedly.

"There are a few more steps, but that's it in a

nutshell," boomed Mrs. Gold above the noise. "If you'll excuse me, I have to make a few phone calls. I'll be back in about fifteen minutes. They should be done by then." Alex, Ray, and Amy nodded, then turned back to the press.

"Hey, Al." Alex turned to Ray as he yelled over the press. She could just barely hear him. "Those old rollers are huge!" he said, pointing toward the older printing press's barrel-like rollers in the back. Alex nodded, then turned to Amy so she could point out the rollers.

Amy was leafing through several stacks of newspapers and bulletins sitting on the floor close to the belt that carried the newsletter to its finish. Alex watched as Amy bent over to go through the next pile and in the process knocked over a fist-size can of black ink on a shelf with her elbow. Amy seemed totally oblivious. She was still looking at the stack of newspapers.

But Alex and Ray weren't oblivious. As they watched in horror, the can slowly rolled across a table toward the printing press, heading right for a long tube next to the newsletter!

Alex started to panic, realizing the top of the can wasn't on tightly. There was only one thing to do: use her telekinetic power to stop the moving can.

Looking around, she noticed that Mike and Joe had gone into a back office and no one else was in sight. As she turned toward Amy, the English girl looked over at Alex and smiled, still oblivious to the moving can of ink. Amy pointed to the newspaper in her hand, then opened it to the first page, turning her back on Alex and Ray. *Great*, thought Alex, *now I can—*

But it was too late. The container had traveled down the table, right into a tube near the printing press, and toward the conveyor belt. She had to catch it before it popped out on the newsletter!

Alex pointed to the tube and Ray nodded, yelling something that was lost in the printing press noise. Alex pulled Ray toward a building beam. Moving forward, she stood with the beam between her, Amy, and the door. She mouthed the words, "You watch." Ray nodded, comprehending. If anyone came through any of the doors or offices, or if Amy turned around, she could count on Ray to keep them occupied.

Alex concentrated, morphing into a silvery liquid puddle. She headed for the press, slipping in and out of the cans of ink, stacks of paper, and piles of towels on the floor. Slithering up a thin pole, Alex oozed into the tube. She noticed that she should be just in time. The slow moving ink can was just about to fall on the press!

Alex made a gurgling noise, then strained to catch up with the ink can. Pacing herself with the moving can, she leaned to the right and nudged the container in another direction. As Alex watched, the small can rolled through the end of the tube and fell harmlessly to the ground, its cover intact. "Whew!" she muttered to herself as she watched the container come to a stop.

Alex looked around, realizing the only way back to Ray was to slide down the pole in front of her. As she rolled down, she landed on the newsletter traveling down the conveyor belt. Looking around, she smiled. *Cool,* she thought, riding down the belt.

Ray gritted his teeth and tried to look nonchalant, but Alex, in liquid form, was starting to head for the folding part of the press!

CHAPTER 8

Alex watched calmly as she was carried down the press. Then, looking ahead, she saw the metal bars folding the pages of the newsletter. "Uh, oh!" she gurgled. Looking back, she saw Ray motioning frantically toward the office in the back. Mike and Joe were coming back toward the press!

"Hey, Mike." Above all the noise, Alex heard Joe call to the foreman. The young assistant looked over in her direction. "Something strange on the press. Looks like some type of liquid."

Mike turned to Ray, who shrugged. "Hey! Did you kids touch the press?" he yelled. Ray shook his head vigorously. Amy looked up from her newspaper and shook her head. Mike motioned to Joe and turned to the switch box across the room. "Stop the press!" he yelled to the technician.

As the press began to slow, Alex slid down the side of a conveyor belt and out of sight. She slipped around a stack of papers, along the side of the press, and behind a beam. With no one in sight, she reformed quickly. Catching her breath, she looked around her. She had to do something to take their minds off the "liquid" around the press.

Sitting on the ground was another can of ink with a small brush inside. Gritting her teeth, she took the brush and splashed it against the front of her white- and light brown-striped T-shirt. *Glad this is an old T-shirt,* she thought, looking at the mess on her shirt. She took a deep breath and stepped from behind the beam.

"Oh, I can't believe it," she said, looking down at her shirt. "This is one of my favorite T-shirts!"

Mike and Joe turned to her and laughed. "One thing you'll learn about the press is that the ink gets everywhere," said Mike, holding up his own stained hands. "Over there, on that sink." He pointed to a sink on Alex's left. "Use that greasy looking stuff on the sink near the faucet. It should take it off pretty well."

Alex looked over at the jar and made a face. It looked a little too greasy for her taste. "Thanks, but I'll just wait until I get back to school. I think my friend has an extra shirt in her locker."

"Suit yourself," Mike said, shrugging and turning back to the press. Both he and Joe took off their caps and scratched their heads. Alex thought they were probably wondering if Joe really *did* see liquid on the press. And she wasn't going to volunteer the real answer.

As Alex reached Ray, she rolled her eyes. Looking over in Amy's direction, Alex whispered to Ray, "Do you think she saw—"

"All right!" came a booming voice, as the back door flew open. "Once the ink's dry, you—what happened to you?" said Mrs. Gold, stopping in midsentence and looking at Alex's shirt.

"I was looking for a bathroom when I found a can of ink instead," Alex said. "But it's okay. A friend of mine has an extra shirt back at school," she added, when she noticed the panicky look on Mrs. Gold's face.

Jake's mother regained her smile and started gathering up copies of the newsletter. "Well, here it is. All ready to hand out. We put it through a special drier that dries the ink faster. They should be completely dry by now."

Alex smiled as Mrs. Gold handed her and Ray the pages. "We can't thank you enough. And I'll be sure to write up an article about your press for the next newsletter."

Mrs. Gold let out a loud laugh. "Great! I've always wanted to be in a newspaper. Printing one is sort of the next best thing, right?"

Alex and Ray turned toward the doors, juggling the pages in their hands. Now all they had to do was staple the pages together when they got back to school. As they walked through the door, Amy stopped to thank Mrs. Gold. Ray leaned over to Alex. "Whew. That was too close, Al," he said as walked out of earshot from Amy and Mrs. Gold.

Alex nodded in agreement. "I guess that's one way of stopping the presses," she whispered to her friend, "but not one I'd like to try again."

* * *

"Hot off the press," called Ray as students passed him in the hall on the way to sixth period. Everyone in Alex's group, and Amy, was distributing the paper in the hallways, giving copies to teachers and putting stacks on shelves in the cafeteria and library and at the principal's office.

As she looked down at her T-shirt, Alex felt almost human again. Robyn, who carried everything in her purse—and if it wasn't there, it was in her locker—did have an extra T-shirt. It was black and Alex didn't like the rock group pictured on the front, but it didn't really matter. It just felt good to be out of the ink-splattered T-shirt.

Alex watched happily as students grabbed the newsletters, reading them as they walked to class. It felt good to hear a few words like, "Wow" and "Hey, I didn't know that," as people passed her in the hall.

"Hey, Alex," came the familiar voice of Nicole. "Nice job."

Alex turned to her friend and smiled. It was

good hearing such a comment from someone on Emily's team, especially Nicole. "Yeah, isn't it great. You should hear all the great comments."

"Yeah, but, Alex—"

"Mr. Granger said he wanted some extra copies to send to a friend of his in Canada," Alex went on excitedly.

"Alex, I think you should know—"

"And not only that, Nicole. Do you remember the—" Alex hesitated and looked down at the papers cradled in her friend's left arm. It definitely wasn't Alex's newsletter. "Umm. What's that you're holding, Nicole?"

"That's what I've been trying to tell you, Alex," she said, smiling and holding up the stack of papers. "This is *our* latest newsletter—hot off the press, as Ray would say. That's number two." She pulled out a copy of the newsletter from the pile. "Isn't this great?"

Alex didn't know what to say. She stood there as Nicole pushed the computer group's newsletter into her free hand. As Nicole walked away, distributing her newsletter, Alex shook her head. First it was Emily, and now it seemed as if some of her best friends were against her, too.

"Al. Hey, Al!" Ray came running up to Alex, almost knocking her down. "Did you see?" he asked, holding up his copy of the other group's newsletter. Robyn and Amy walked up, staring at the paper in Ray's hand.

"Yeah," she said, holding up the copy Nicole had given her.

"Did you read it—especially the second story?" he asked, his eyes wide.

As Robyn and Amy leaned over her shoulder, Alex read the second story halfway down the page and frowned. There was a photo of an older man dressed in a suit and a bow tie. The caption read, "Mr. Bart Gibson has invented a new chemical to get rid of termites," and below was an article about him by Emily Baker.

"You've been pipped at the post, Ray," Amy exclaimed, shaking her head.

Ray looked at her. "If you mean they beat me again at a story, you're right. Mr. Gibson told me he hadn't told anyone else about his invention," Ray protested, "and I just talked with him this morning!"

"Wait a minute, Ray," said Alex, still frowning. "Did you tell anyone else?"

Ray shook his head.

"Maybe Emily really did a good job investigating," suggested Amy, shrugging.

As Ray started to reply, the bell rang for the start of class. As Robyn and Ray raced down the hall toward class, Alex gathered up several newsletters and stuffed them into her backpack. *Or maybe Emily had some help,* she thought, even more concerned, watching Amy head off to the library.

Hi, Alex,
Sorry about the gap in e-mail. Homework, you know! Great news about your first newsletter! And I have faith in you, Alex—they can't go wrong with you as their fearless leader. Remember that creative writing class I (kind of) took once at the local college? I did learn something—that accuracy counts, not to mention a good story! You *better* not use you-know-what around anyone. And stop showing people my desk in the garage—I don't want to see everything in a shambles when I get back this summer. My roommate is back from the infirmary. I was sneezing earlier this morning.

I hope I'm not catching the flu. I have a big science test tomorrow, and I don't want to break my A average. Did Mom really send the Girl Scout cookies? They aren't here yet, and the natives are getting restless. . . . Happy hunt-and-pecking on the typewriter. Love, Annie

CHAPTER 9

Dear Annie,
Having a wonderful time. Wish you were here. . . . I'm beat. . . . Love, Alex

"I don't know about you, but I'm absolutely knackered tonight," said Amy, folding up the latest issue of the *Times,* and straightening her long black skirt.

Alex and Robyn sat in the backseat of the Mack car and Amy sat in front, as Mr. Mack drove them to the observatory. Alex had hurried home from school and grabbed a quick sandwich for dinner. Then she raced upstairs to her room, changed into her good blue jeans and blue striped blouse with the white collar. She had just enough time to prepare her photo equipment, checking on the batteries in the 35-millimeter camera and flash, cleaning off the lenses with a special cleaning cloth, and making sure she had enough film. This was the part Alex liked about working on the newsletter, taking photos, trying to decide on the best angle and if there was enough light, and using that new film everyone was talking about.

Mr. Mack stopped at a traffic light, then turned to the English girl. "Knackered? Sounds like something you eat."

Amy laughed. "It means I'm exhausted. I know. I keep using terms I'm familiar with and forget that not everyone knows what I'm saying. Sorry."

Robyn leaned forward in her seat. "Yeah, tonight before dinner, she was 'peckish,' and I figured out she was hungry. Because so was I. Then after dinner, she was 'chuffed.' I thought she meant stuffed, but, no, she meant she was happy. Then she couldn't find her 'plimsolls' before we left, and I was completely in the dark about that."

"Quite. I sometimes forget you call them sneakers over here," replied Amy, turning to Alex and Robyn, then back to Mr. Mack. "It all evens out, though. Sometimes, I have no idea what all of *you* are saying."

Mr. Mack laughed, then turned as he started the car moving again. "One of the people I work with at Paradise Valley Chemical is from England. He told me it took him almost six months to get used to the way we talk. And you've only been here a few days. Well, here we are, ladies. The taxi ride ends here for now."

Alex, Robyn, and Amy hopped out of the car. "Check, Dad. Thanks for the ride. We'll see you later," Alex said, hiking the camera bag higher on her shoulder.

As Mr. Mack drove away, the three girls stopped on the sidewalk. Alex looked up and noticed there wasn't a cloud in the sky—perfect for observing the stars and the new comet through the telescope. The observatory was actually two buildings. One was about half the size of her school and, as Ray had told her earlier, housed the astronomer's offices. The other was the actual observatory, complete with a silver observatory dome. Alex thought it looked like something out of a science fiction movie. *After all, you don't see domed buildings every day,* she thought.

They all jumped as the dome suddenly started to move, turning slowly toward the left. As it moved, a small gap opened in the dome.

"Did we miss the show?" Robyn said over the sound of the motor.

Suddenly the front door to the attached building opened and out stepped Ray. "Hey, guys, over here!"

Alex and the others walked up to Ray. "How did you get here so fast? And what happened to Mr. Gibson?"

"Aw, I decided not to bother," he said. "I called him earlier and he told me he was sorry, but someone called him earlier in the day saying she was working on a newsletter. He assumed it was someone working with me, so he gave the interview."

"Did he say who it was?" asked Alex, knowing the answer already.

"Yeah, our friend Emily. Mr. Gibson called her a very nice girl with a pleasant voice. More like a very sneaky girl with a squeaky voice."

Robyn stifled a laugh.

"Oh, I don't know," Amy said. "We had a nice natter today. She's all right."

"Natter?" asked Ray, scratching his head. "Sounds like a candy bar."

Robyn rolled her eyes. "No, it means chat. Right?" Amy nodded. "I'm getting the hang of this now, Amy. Bung me another word."

"Enough bunging for now, guys," interrupted Alex. Even though she was dying to ask Amy what she and Emily were talking about, this wasn't the time. They had an interview to do. She pointed to the observatory. "We're going to be late if we don't start moving."

"How perfectly banger of me," replied Robyn, faking a curtsy and then stepping through the door.

"Banger is a sausage, Robyn," Amy corrected. Robyn shrugged.

The observatory was nothing like how Alex had pictured it. In the movies, telescopes always seemed to be in brightly lit offices, and all the astronomer had to do was look into an eyepiece at the bottom of the telescope. But the real observatory was very different. The room was circular and was about as wide as the Macks' kitchen. There was a console against a side wall from which the dome and telescope were run. Ray wrote furiously in his notebook as Dr. Cooke explained that the room was bathed in red light so the astronomers could see better. Regular light made it hard to see, the way it is hard to see the stars when you've come outside from a brightly lit house.

Alex stared at the telescope as Dr. Cooke swung it toward the open gap in the observatory dome. It was one of the longest tubes she had ever seen, and the place you looked into was only as wide as one of her film containers. Dr. Cooke moved the telescope so they could all see the new comet. As Alex stood on her toes to look into the viewfinder, she could hardly believe it: there was a fuzzy dot followed by a long white tail. "It looks just like the photos I've seen on television and in the newspapers, only better," she said to Dr. Cooke. She moved back as Robyn and Amy took their turns at the telescope.

The astronomer laughed. "Doesn't everything—and everyone—look better in person?"

Ray shook his head as he took Amy's place at the telescope. "You haven't seen B. B. Pearson, have you?" Dr. Cooke shook his head. "He's got my vote for the all-time best linebacker to come out of Paradise High. Looks just as scary in his pictures as he does on the field. And he's almost as round as this comet," Ray added, gazing into the telescope. Robyn snickered and Alex rolled her eyes.

"Take as many pictures as you like, Alex," said Dr. Cooke, turning toward Alex as he stepped away from the telescope. "You'll probably want to take one of the telescope, the console, and the open dome—maybe with the telescope in the foreground."

"Can I get a shot of you?" she asked, holding up her camera.

"Yes, after I give Ray his interview," he pointed to the doors in the back of the observatory. "We'll be in the first office down on the left if you need us."

" 'Scuse me, can I have this newsletter?" asked

Amy, picking up the observatory's bulletin from a nearby bench.

"Sure, help yourself," answered Dr. Cooke. "There's some information on the comet in there, too."

As Ray and Dr. Cooke walked to the office, Alex moved over near Robyn and pushed a few buttons on her camera. "Want to be in some of the shots? So our readers can see how big the telescope is compared to a human?"

"Me? Oh, gee, Alex," said Robyn, straightening her short black skirt, then raking her hand through her hair. "I wish you had said something before we came. I'll be back. Just let me put my hair in a bun. I can't stand it when I see a picture of myself with my hair hanging down like a stringy mess. Especially if I'm wearing a skirt."

"Robyn, it looks fine. *You* look fine," protested Alex. "I'll take the pictures from far away so no one will know it's you."

"*I'll* know it's me. I'll just be a minute," said Robyn, grabbing her purse and running out the back door.

Alex turned to Amy. "You want to be in a shot?"

"Not without my theater makeup," she answered, smiling.

"All right, everyone," said Alex, turning back to her camera. "I get the hint."

Alex walked around the telescope, trying to decide what the best angle would be to take the photo. As she reached in her camera bag for her flash, Alex heard something *swoosh,* then squeak behind her.

"Oops!"

Alex's eyes went wide. Turning, she saw Amy trip, then fall toward the far wall, right near two large buttons. As Amy reached out to steady herself, Alex saw her hit the green button. Then the huge observatory dome began to move rapidly around in a circle!

"My jumper," cried Amy as the observatory dome continued to spin. Dropping her camera into her case, Alex ran to Amy's side. Her black sweater had caught on a small hook attached to the observatory dome, lifting her up and carrying her around the room. "Alex!"

Alex stopped and started to concentrate, knowing that she could stop the spinning dome with her telekinetic power. But that was too dangerous.

She didn't know what would happen to the dome's motor if she did try to stop it from moving. More importantly, Amy would definitely see Alex use her powers. "Hold on, Amy! I'll get Dr. Cooke!"

Running out the door and into the hall, Alex started yelling. "Dr. Cooke. Where are you?"

Dr. Cooke stuck his head out an office doorway. "What's wrong?"

"The dome, it's spinning and Amy is, too!"

Dr. Cooke turned inside the office and said something to Ray, then came running down the hall past Alex. With Alex and Ray at his heels, he pushed his way into the observatory and raced to the controls. As he turned several switches and pushed a button, nothing happened. Amy was still spinning along with the observatory dome.

Alex looked at Ray and nodded. Noticing that Dr. Cooke was busy with the controls, Alex headed for the outside of the dome and onto the flat roof. Racing around the side of the dome, she saw what she was looking for: a fuse box. Standing on her toes, she strained to see the words on the front of the box. D. O. M. E. Dome motor! she read. She turned to the left and right, making sure no one was around. *I hope this works,* she thought, *and it only turns off the dome. I don't know how I'd explain it if all the power went out.* She stood back, aimed her right finger at the metal box and zapped it. Sparks flew everywhere. As the box sizzled and fizzled, the dome came to a screeching halt.

"Dr. Cooke," she said, running back into the dome. Ray was helping Amy to sit down in a nearby chair. The astronomer was standing over his control panel, scratching his head. "Dr. Cooke," she said again, "I think your fuse box is frazzled. It's a mess. Maybe that's what happened." Amy looked over at Alex, surprised.

Dr. Cooke mumbled, then turned to Alex. "Ummm. Yes," he finally said. "Maybe so. Strangest thing, though." He turned to Ray and let out a sigh. "Well, young man, I'm afraid that's it for the interview. I think I should check this out before I do anything else. I can give you an interview another day."

"But I—" Ray started to protest, then hesitated, realizing the astronomer was right. "Yes, sir. Some other time."

Alex, Ray, and Amy picked up their backpacks

and walked to the front of the observatory to wait for Mr. Mack. "Bye, bye, big story," said Ray, slamming his notebook.

"I'm really sorry, Ray," said Amy, standing above Alex and Ray and shaking her head. "I'm pretty clumsy. I went a bit wonky and accidentally hit a button on the wall." She turned to Alex. "I know I did it. It wasn't the fuse box. Why did you tell Dr. Cooke that?"

"Because when I went outside, it was frazzled," said Alex. She wasn't lying. The box was a mess, especially after she zapped it.

Ray sighed and looked down at the ground. "Don't worry about it. I think I got a few things out of the interview. But I'll have to go to the library tomorrow and dig up some information on astronomy to fill in the story. I just wish I could use the computer. I could get it done tonight."

Amy tsked, then sat down next to Alex. But something was bothering Alex. It sure seemed as if there had been too many "accidents" lately, and those accidents often put Alex's newsletter group behind the other group. Was Amy working for Emily? It sounded like something Emily would do. After all, she didn't know much about

Amy except that she was a friend of Robyn's family.

They all turned as someone walked up behind them. "Hey, guys. Where did you all go?" asked Robyn, her hair now in a tight bun.

Alex looked at Ray and sighed. "Have a seat, Robyn," replied Alex. "It's a long story."

Dear Rodney and Randy: You both *have* the "Taco Terror"??? I can't believe that Aunt Janet would get you that game! Cool! I've managed to put out that wonderful newsletter—oh, with the help of some of the people in my group, of course. But everyone is talking about my stories. I knew I had the writing knack before. As I told you, I used to be a columnist for our junior high school paper, the Atomizer. Some of us are just born great. Then again, one girl in our group is really pushy, even more than I am. I don't really like the way she does things, but she's the group leader, and the newsletter does get out fast. So it looks like we're going to win! Well, it's time for these fancy fingers to type the next fantastic article. Louis the G.

CHAPTER 10

Hi, Alex,
I will be spending the rest of this week in the infirmary. Yes, I caught my roommate's flu. (I'm using the rest of my strength to type to you—see what a wonderful sister I am?) I told Mom it was because we got the cookies too late. Oh, and I just remembered—the stupid tennis racket is in the attic. Love, Annie

It was a long, restless night for Alex. She knew that the other group was faster because they had computers, but she was suspicious of Emily and her scoops and anonymous sources. Early in the morning she realized she had to do something for her group, and that meant talking to Emily. As she and Ray walked to school, she told him her plan. He volunteered to go, and she accepted. She wanted Robyn to come along, too. The three of them would confront Emily and tell her that all the scoops were enough already.

As Alex, Ray, and Robyn, along with Amy, stood outside the computer center, Louis ran out the door, nodding to them curtly. "Another big scoop, and Louis the Great is on it," he said, pulling a pencil from behind his ear. Ray rolled his eyes at Alex, then shook his head. Alex could tell Ray didn't understand why his good friend was being so dorky.

As they entered the computer room, there was chaos everywhere. Two girls were scanning photos into a scanner, while two other boys were scrambling around, stacking page after page together, then pressing the pages into a binding machine. Alex thought it looked almost as busy as the printer's, except there was not as much noise.

Nicole was typing rapidly on a computer keyboard, a pencil clamped between her teeth. "Em-ree. Do oo-ave-a—" Nicole tried to say.

"I can't understand you with the pencil in your mouth," retorted Emily, staring intently at her own computer screen. She pushed up the sleeves of her red blouse.

Nicole spit out the pencil. "Do you have the Internet address for the local university?"

As Alex walked closer, Emily hit a few buttons on the keyboard, but not before Alex read the word *Observatory* in the headline on Emily's computer monitor. "Check the World Wide Web address on one of those search engines," replied Emily. "Now why can't I— Oh, hello, Mack," she said, frowning as she noticed Alex for the first time. She got up, ignoring the others, and stood in front of Alex. "You're just the person I wanted to see."

"Me?" Alex asked, truly puzzled. "I thought I was the one with the questions."

"Me first. I think we better get something straight, Mack. Someone is cheating on this assignment, and I think I know who it is," Emily said, putting her hands on her hips.

Ray started to move forward, but Alex held

him back. "Go on," Alex said, trying to hold back her own anger. She felt as if her face were as red as Emily's blouse.

"This morning, when we were about to print out some of the latest newsletter," continued Emily, "the laser printer wouldn't print out the fonts, or kinds of type, we wanted. It just spit out some gibberish that no one could read."

"And you think I had something to do with that?" asked Alex, crossing her arms in front of her.

"Yeah. Because we found out later that the font card, the one that tells the computer what type of font to type, was missing. Somebody swiped it," she said, scowling at Alex. "Mrs. Marvin got permission for us to use the principal's electric typewriter," she added. Alex thought Emily shivered when she mentioned the word *typewriter*.

"So what's wrong with that?" asked Amy, tapping her right foot with her chunky, black shoe.

"Oh, it looks all right, but I would have preferred my laser printer," answered Emily. "And not only that, the scanner light went out yesterday, just before we were going to scan in a photo. We had to photocopy the picture, then *paste* it into the newsletter. I couldn't believe it. That's why I'm suspicious, Mack. Too much of a coincidence."

"You're still putting out your newsletter faster than we are," noted Ray, shaking his head at Emily.

"Sure. But it's been rough. Maybe we'll get more points because we had to rely on—on your way," said Emily, still scowling. "I told Mrs. Marvin what happened. I could tell she was on our side."

Ray snorted.

"Very doubtful, Emily," replied Robyn. "And it's more likely you forgot where you put the card. And the light just went out naturally."

"Nice try, Robyn. But, you know, I don't hold a grudge," said Emily, turning again to Alex. "Now why are you here?"

"We just want to know—" started Alex.

"How I get my information?" asked Emily, finishing Alex's sentence. "How did I know what you were after? It's very easy. I'm a good reporter. And a good reporter digs. I have good intuition."

"But isn't accuracy important?" asked Amy, tilting her head.

"I put down the facts as I hear and read them. That's good reporting. And when I type it in the computer, the machine checks me for grammar and spelling. So as far as I'm concerned, my text is fine. The computer says so; I say so." Emily sat back down in her chair and grabbed the computer mouse in her right hand. As she moved the mouse, she read the screen and smiled. "Speaking of reporting, my group just wrote a story about the new comet and the local observatory. We just e-mailed the astronomer and downloaded the photos from the Internet. Don't worry. You'll read about it in tomorrow's edition. Now, if you'll all excuse me. I have to get this done before next period." She began typing text again into the computer. "Okay, Terry. Put this on the front page," she called to a girl across the room.

Realizing she was getting nowhere, Alex turned to the others and motioned to the door. It was hard, but Alex kept her cool. After all, the last thing she wanted to do was get mad or nervous and start glowing in front of Emily. *That would be giving Emily one scoop I really couldn't afford,* she thought.

That night Alex was exhausted again. It was time to attend the reading of her mother's play in front of Mrs. Hutton. To Alex's left sat Amy and Robyn, sitting with the Russos. On Alex's right were her parents.

Even though Alex's conversation with Emily had been a bust, she was much calmer. After all, the next newsletter was almost done. After school, while Amy typed a note on the Macks' laptop to her friend in England, and her mother printed out the latest version of her script, Alex and Robyn pasted most of the photos and articles into the newsletter. Alex smiled as she thought of Robyn's latest contribution, a story about the fight to stop officials at Paradise High from cutting down the huge old pine tree in front of the school, a tree that contained a red squirrel's nest. *Emily couldn't have possibly found out about it yet, either,* she thought, satisfied.

As Alex settled in her seat, she looked around the college auditorium. It was filled with students and parents, all eager to hear Mrs. Hutton's critiques of the drama class scripts.

The audience clapped after the first script was read. As Mrs. Hutton talked to the students and the rest of the audience about the play, Mrs. Mack fiddled nervously with the collar on her light yellow dress. Alex leaned over and smoothed out the collar, then took Mrs. Mack's hand. She knew what it was like to have to speak in front of others. After all, she had had to read several of her papers this year in front of her English class, and just the thought of it made her palms sweat. "Mom, everything's going to be all right. They'll love it, really."

"Now *you* sound like the mother," whispered Mrs. Mack. She smiled and squeezed Alex's hand. "Yes, this too shall pass."

"Barbara Mack?" said Mr. Donaldson, the drama professor. Mrs. Mack released Alex's hand and stood up. As the professor introduced her to the audience, Mrs. Mack walked carefully up the side stairs and onto the stage. The audience applauded as Mr. Donaldson adjusted the microphone to Mrs. Mack's height, and Alex let out a whistle in support of her mother.

Mrs. Mack smiled and flipped open the folder

holding her script. Looking out over the audience, she took a deep breath. "Thank you all. The title of my script is *The Middle of Somewhere.*" She cleared her throat softly and turned to the first page. " 'What happens when they cut down the huge pine tree in front of Paradise High? We'll lose a red squirrel's nest for—one—thing—' What in the—"

Alex's eyes went wide—and her mother's eyes went even wider. Mrs. Mack looked up, confused. Alex immediately recognized the first few words of the sentence. It was Robyn's new story for the first page of the newsletter!

"Oh, I'm terribly sorry," Mrs. Mack was saying, sifting through the pages in search of her manuscript. "I don't know what happened, Mr. Donaldson. Umm, Mrs. Hutton. Please forgive me. I must have copied the wrong file. Or something." Mrs. Mack looked up from the papers and stared down at Alex.

As Alex scrunched down in her seat, she felt her stomach lurch. She had never touched the computer for her newsletter! How did Robyn's story get in there?

* * *

"Come on, come on."

Alex watched as Ray tried to coax the electric typewriter to type another letter. As he hit a key, the machine hesitated, then banged the peg into the paper to type a letter. It was just before school started, and Alex, Ray, Sara-Jo, and Robyn, along with Amy, had agreed to meet and type out the rest of the newsletter. Mr. Mack volunteered to drop Alex and Ray off at school with the typewriters on his way to work, and Mrs. Marvin had agreed to allow Alex and her group to put the typewriters in the computer center, where there were plenty of tables to work on.

Alex was feeling a little better than she had the night before. Her mother was already up when Alex came down for breakfast. As Alex wolfed down a bagel and some cereal, she explained to her mother that she hadn't touched the computer yesterday. Her mother believed her. Mrs. Mack said it was her own fault for not checking the printout, and that Mrs. Hutton said she'd listen to Mrs. Mack read the script in a few days. But both Alex and her mother were puzzled as to how the article got into the Macks' laptop.

Because she was feeling better, Alex was psyched to finish the newsletter before school started. This time, she knew they'd beat Emily to a scoop. All they needed to do was type in a little more text about the red squirrels and paste in a few pictures.

For some reason—maybe just because they had moved the old electric typewriter from the Macks' house to school—the machine wasn't working right. "At this rate, we'll be done by next semester," said Alex.

"Hey!" Ray shouted in mock anger, turning from the electric typewriter. As Alex watched, Ray accidentally hit the space bar on the machine. Suddenly, the type ball went crazy. It moved quickly all the way over to the right and stayed there. Ray turned around and hit the space bar again, but the type ball still kept to the right. The typewriter's motor was humming furiously. Ray started hitting all the other keys, hoping something would work. Then he moved his hands away from the typewriter as it started to rock back and forth. "Hey, what—"

Suddenly the typewriter stopped. Alex looked up and saw Mrs. Marvin standing behind the desk, the plug to the typewriter in her hand. She pointed to Sara-Jo typing on the manual typewriter. "Maybe you should stick with the old-fashioned manual."

"Yeah," said Amy, pointing to the electric typewriter. "Looks like they sucked the life out of that poor thing."

"Don't worry. You kids are doing a great job," said Mrs. Marvin, looking over the latest pages sitting on the desk. "And you've done it all the old-fashioned way. If this were a computer," she said, pointing to the broken typewriter, "you'd be sunk right now. But you can continue because you have a manual typewriter. Think of it that way. And, Alex, wasn't it you who said sometimes things need the human touch?"

Alex grimaced.

"Here, here!" Amy said, nodding at Mrs. Marvin.

As Alex started to answer, the door to the computer center burst open, and Jake and Dave come running in. Jake was holding several papers in his hand. "Look, everybody! It's the other group's newsletter. That's number three!"

Alex looked over at Mrs. Marvin and sighed.

Dave handed his copy to Alex and pointed to an article on the front page. "Look—the same thing we're writing about in our newsletter, the red squirrel in the pine tree out front."

"Now why doesn't that surprise me," said Robyn, looking over Alex's shoulder.

Alex scanned the page. "Yeah, and they never mention that the pine tree is dead and is a hazard to anyone who walks past the tree."

Amy read the newsletter over Alex's shoulder. "Are you kidding me? She didn't write about that? Daft. Just daft," she added, shaking her head.

The bell rang for the next class. As everyone scattered, Alex walked quickly up to Ray and pulled him aside. "Ray, we have to do something. The other group keeps beating us with the stories. Or should I say, Emily's beating us with her stories. I know you're not leaking the stuff, right?"

Ray looked at Alex, surprised. "You think I'd tell? Hey, you're talking to your best buddy here."

Alex smiled and patted her friend on the shoulder. "Yeah, I know. Listen, Ray. Drop a few hints about our next newsletter when you pass between classes, especially when you see Emily. Tell everyone we have the coolest story of the year and that we're typing it after study hall. Oh, and mention that we keep all our research at the computer center. Then meet me there during study hall. Mrs. Marvin said she'd give us passes. I think it's time we set a little trap for our snooper."

"And you think we'll catch Emily the Red in the act?"

"More like red handed," Alex said, giving Ray the thumbs-up sign as she ran down the hall to her first class.

CHAPTER 11

Alex's mind was racing as she walked to the computer center during study hall. She knew the center would be empty this period, as most of the kids in the computer class had a test then. Alex knew, too, that whoever was scooping her newsletter would definitely want to grab another hot story, and the easier it was to get to, the better. One way or the other, Alex would find out who was leaking all their good stories. Alex was hoping she could prove it was Emily. Maybe by exposing her, they would have a better chance of getting the best grade and the Virtual Reality Center certificates.

Alex and Ray worked furiously to put some old unused photos and stories on a table near the typewriter. "Now what did you say when Emily walked by?" asked Alex, arranging several photos on the table.

"Oh, I was good," said Ray, beaming. "I was telling Roger Rudd about the great story I was writing. I kind of hinted it was about some new computers, and something about playing computer games at school, just to make it exciting. You could see Emily's ears getting larger as we talked."

"But they don't allow computer games on the school's computers."

"I know. That's why I also said they may change the school policy. You said to make it a cool story. Oh, and the best part? It wasn't only Emily who walked by, it was Louis, too."

"You don't suspect him, do you?" asked Alex, turning to Ray.

He thought for a moment. "No, but sometimes I wonder. Sometimes I think he'd do anything to win."

Alex shrugged, then put the last piece of paper on the desk. "I think that's it." She looked around the room. "You wait over there," she said, pointing to one of the computer cubicles. "Hide in that cubicle. You can't tell if anyone's sitting there. I'll wait in the back behind those boxes."

"You going to morph?" asked Ray in a low voice.

Alex shook her head. "No, but I'll send a zapper toward the light switch when their back is turned. Just enough juice to turn on the lights and scare the person. I hope."

Ray nodded and walked slowly over to the door, while Alex made her way back to the boxes and stood behind the largest one. As Ray turned off the lights, Alex noticed that the only light in the room was the glow from several computer monitors. She could follow Ray's silhouette as he walked over to the hidden cubicle.

It didn't take long for someone to come through the door. Just as Alex expected, whoever it was didn't turn on the lights. As Alex watched, she felt her heart pounding furiously. The culprit walked across the room and headed straight for the papers near the typewriter.

As Alex watched, she could see the silhouette

of the person patting the pages, then looking under the desk. While the person's back was turned, Alex moved quickly from behind the box, then sent a zapper out toward the light switch.

The room suddenly filled with light—and there stood Nicole!

"Nicole!" yelled Alex, coming out from behind the boxes. Nicole jumped and stared at Alex. She was frozen, as Ray would have said, like a deer in a car's headlights.

"Alex! Gee, you scared me! But, boy, am I glad to see you," she said, continuing to pat the table.

Ray sauntered forward toward Nicole. Alex knew that look and braced herself for Ray, Detective mode. "Now, Nicole," he said, scratching his chin. "Just what were you doing in here—and without the lights on?"

"Well, Mr. Prosecutor," she said, moving over and pushing around several books sitting at the desk next to the typewriter. She stood back and put her hands on her hips. "I lost my watch. You know, the silver one my mom gave me for my birthday? I know I took it off this morning when I was at this terminal. It kept hitting the desk when I typed. I didn't turn the lights on because I thought it was right on top here." She eyed Alex and Ray suspiciously. "And what were you two doing in here, anyway?"

Alex didn't know what to say. Here she was ready to blame Nicole for stealing the typewriter group's ideas. How could she tell one of her best friends that she was ready to accuse her of stealing? "Ummm. We were trying an experiment," she said, which was true. After all, seeing if they could catch the person was an experiment. She hadn't really known it would work. "I guess it didn't work."

"Ah, there it is," Nicole said, holding up the silver watch. "Right under these papers. Well, you two just keep up with your little experiment. I've got to run back to the history test."

As Nicole raced out the door, Ray looked at Alex sheepishly. "Are we just paranoid?" he asked, looking down at the papers on the table.

"No, Ray. At least I hope not," she said, fixing the piles of paper Nicole had moved in her attempt to find her watch. "Listen, let's just try it once more. If no one shows in about ten minutes, well, then maybe we can think of something different."

After Ray turned off the lights again, they went back to their hiding places. Alex looked at her watch several times and noticed that the hands on its luminous dial seemed to be moving awfully slowly. She knew it was just because she was waiting. That always seemed to happen.

Just as Alex was about to announce that time was up, she heard the door to the computer center creak open. Someone walked silently across the room and headed for the papers near the typewriter.

This time Alex decided not to turn on the lights as fast. As she watched, the figure gathered up several of the pages from the table, then walked over to one of the lit computers. Setting the papers on the terminal desk, the person grabbed the mouse. Alex crept out from behind the boxes, slowly working her way over to the computer. Out of the corner of her eye, she saw Ray moving forward, too.

Both Alex and Ray stopped and watched. The person activated the computer modem, and began to type in a message to the electronic mail system. Alex slid closer, straining to see the writing on the computer monitor.

The note was addressed to Emily!

The person grabbed the mouse again, but the electronic device slipped to the floor. *"Oops!"* came the voice—one that Alex knew by heart.

The person sitting in the chair was Amy Hutton!

Alex moved quickly behind Ray and turned around. Carefully aiming, she sent a zapper toward the back wall, turning on the lights. Amy jumped and turned around, surprised to see Alex and Ray standing behind her.

"Are you two daft?" she said, holding a hand to her chest and blinking from the sudden brightness. "You almost gave me heart failure."

"Amy, what are you doing here?" asked Alex, walking over to stand next to the English girl.

"Well, I should ask the same of you two," Amy replied, still holding her chest.

Ray started to say something, but Alex held up her hand. "Wait, Ray. We're here to see who wants our stuff," Alex explained. "Now why are you here?"

Amy looked at Alex and Ray, then back at the

computer. She reached down for the mouse, then pushed a few keys, terminating the message she was sending. "Oh, what's the use," she said, leaning back in her chair. "I was trying to help everyone."

"Help? How? By giving away our ideas?" asked Alex.

"No, I didn't," she protested. "Well, yes—but not really," she continued. "You don't know how frustrating it was watching all of you go through this assignment."

"So you're making us all lose because *you're* frustrated?" asked Ray, his voice rising in anger.

"No, well—yes, quite," Amy said, hesitating, then sighing. "All you and your mates talk about," she said, pointing to Ray and Alex, "is not having a computer. I tried to explain to you that you were lucky, that you should be happy with the old-fashioned way. It's not so bad working like that. By giving scoops to Emily, I was hoping it would make you work harder—give you the old adrenaline rush, see how lucky you were to put everything out accurately, do it slowly."

"And all the accidents you had?" asked Alex.

"Oh, those. I'm a bit wonky sometimes," answered Amy, fussing with an earring. "Clumsy, you might say. It's my long arms. They get in the way."

"And what about Emily and her group?" asked Ray.

"Sure, I bunged over a few scoops to Emily, but she found the rest on her own. She's a good investigator, but she's really dotty and falls for everything. Lots of mistakes, if you ask me. I tried to explain that to her a few times, too, but she thought she knew better. She even shivered when I mentioned that she should look something up in a library. So I figured if I fed her some rotten information, and she got it wrong in her newsletter, the next time she'd be more careful. But she wasn't."

Alex shook her head. "But, Amy," she said. "Some one has to get the top mark and the certificates. You were putting us at a real disadvantage."

Amy raised an eyebrow. "Is that all you care about? If you want my opinion, I don't think you're putting out a good newsletter anymore. I think you're balmy about getting certificates and beating Emily, and Emily's balmy about putting out a billion inaccurate newsletters."

Alex sat down heavily in a nearby chair. She suddenly realized that Amy was right. Maybe they were all putting out the newsletters for the wrong reasons.

"So instead of trying to beat Emily and get certificates—" started Ray, leaning on a nearby chair.

"We should be concentrating on writing a better newsletter. Period," Alex said, finishing Ray's thought.

The English girl nodded vigorously. "Don't you see? Both computers and typewriters have their place. Back where I live, all we do is cut and paste, paste and cut," she said, pushing back a stray lock of hair from her forehead. "We don't use the computer, because we don't have that many. I should know. I'm the editor of my school's newspaper." She hesitated, then held up the *Times*. "I guess that's why I carry around all these newspapers. They're for study."

"Really? You're the editor?" asked Alex. "Why didn't you say something?"

Amy seemed to snort. "It probably wouldn't

have made any difference anyway," she answered. "You are all so obsessed about not having a computer. Don't you see that you can learn so much more, and put out a smashing newsletter, by going slower? You know the old story—my mum used to tell it to me. The one about the tortoise and the hare."

Alex smiled at the reference to the fable. "Yeah, the hare does everything fast, trying to get to the finish line, and the tortoise takes his time and wins."

Amy nodded in reply. "You're right, Amy," Alex said, sighing. "I guess we were kind of focusing on not having a computer." *And I was focusing on Emily*, she thought.

Amy nodded. "You know me. Like I told you. It's what my mum does—always trying to help people, teach them the lessons of life."

Alex nodded. "And we didn't listen before when you said we should concentrate on quality not quantity."

"That would be a great editorial, Alex," said Amy. "Oh, and I might mention your mum's script, Alex. Remember how I was sending the electronic mail to my friend back in England the other night while you worked on the newsletter? I sent her a copy of the red squirrel story. When I got out of the e-mail program, I must have hit the wrong button and saved it in you mum's file that held the script. Don't ask me how. I know some about computers, but sometimes, they really, really mystify me. Sorry about that."

Alex put her hand on Amy's shoulder. "Next time, let one of us know. We'll help." She shook her head, realizing what a dork she had been. "Amy, thanks for your—well, help, I guess, but, really, you could have just told us. We really would have listened."

"Fat chance of that. I did try. But when no one was listening, I decided to do something about it—until you caught me, that is," she said, looking at the computer.

"Well, we still have a fighting chance. Amy, will you help us with the next newsletter? And will you do an interview with me?" Alex asked. As Amy smiled and nodded, Alex turned to Ray. "Great. Meeting tonight, Ray. I want everyone over at my house to work on the newsletter. Let's go spread the word."

Amy stood up, then turned to Alex. "Listen, maybe if I just bung a little note to Emily—"

Alex shook her head. "No, I'm chuffed the way things are."

Amy put her arm around Alex's shoulder as they both laughed. "I'll teach you to be an Englishwoman yet."

CHAPTER 12

. . . and what did this assignment mean to me? Probably more than anything, it was an education in how to put out a good, accurate newsletter, one that everyone in Paradise High would enjoy. It wasn't about the number of newsletters we put out, or what we used—computers, typewriters, or pen and ink—to compose the newsletters. In other words, it all came down to quality, not quantity.

In the past two weeks, I also learned a great deal from our recent visitor, Amy Hutton from England, a friend of the Russo family and the editor of her school newspaper back home. Amy has traveled all over the world with her famous mother, the playwright, Lucy Hutton. "And in our travels,

I've seen people do wonderful things," says Amy, "create wonderful ideas, just with a pen and paper. In other places, computers are everywhere, and still wonderful ideas are created." Amy's whole point is that all the resources around us are important,and we should use *all* of them to the best of our ability.

I think we all learned many lessons from this assignment. And, because of that, I think both newsletter teams won.

Alex Mack, Editor

Mrs. Marvin smiled as she set down the newsletter. "That was the latest editorial from the *PH Times* newsletter. I want you all to know that this is one of the most inspirational editorials I've ever read. Alex, you did a wonderful job."

Alex blushed, then turned to the members of her group and Amy. "I couldn't have done it without them."

"Well, it is your editorial," she said. "Class, based on what I've seen, read, and the comments I have received from the rest of the students and faculty, I'm giving Alex Mack's group the top grade for the newsletter assignment."

As Alex, Robyn, and Amy stood up and

hugged one another, the rest of the group cheered. Emily raised her hand, waving frantically.

"Yes, Emily?" said Mrs. Marvin, pointing to Emily.

The cheers quieted down and everyone stopped to listen. "Mrs. Marvin. How can they win?" asked Emily. "We put out two more newsletters than they did. We wrote more stories than they did. I think this is unfair," she added. Only one person in her group cheered her on. Alex noticed both Nicole and Louis remained silent. *Maybe they figured out Emily had her own agenda after all,* Alex thought, smiling.

"I know, Emily. You did put out more words and newsletters," explained Mrs. Marvin. "But did you hear what Alex's editorial said? It's not quantity, it's quality."

As Emily started to protest, Alex stood up. "Mrs. Marvin, there was one thing I'd like to emphasize from my editorial." Alex looked at Amy, then turned back to Mrs. Marvin. "I think everyone should get an A."

Alex heard Emily gasp.

"Is there a reason for your request, Alex?" asked Mrs. Marvin.

"We all learned something valuable here, Mrs. Marvin," she explained. "Isn't that what this was supposed to be? We learned that computers are great, but so are things that require—the human touch?" she added, smiling.

"Good point, Alex. So be it," said Mrs. Marvin, opening up her grade book. "Everyone gets an A and the certificates to the Virtual Reality Center."

As cheering from all around erupted, Alex looked over at Emily. She squinted at Alex, shook her head, then smiled broadly at Alex and waved. Alex smiled back, waving, then turned to hug the others in her group.

The front doorbell rang, and Alex sprang up from her bed. "I got it!" she yelled, running down the stairs to answer the door. As she swung the door open, Buster pushed his snout into the room and started sniffing a nearby magazine rack.

"Oops! Sorry, Alex," said Amy, pulling on Buster's leash. "He's a bit of a bruiser, isn't he?"

Robyn walked in with her aunt's two cats and smiled. Alex thought she looked like the proverbial cat who swallowed the canary. "Hey, I'm not a glutton for punishment. I gave Buster to Amy today."

Alex laughed. "I told Mom I was helping you walk the animals today, but I have to be back in about an hour. I'm going to play tennis with Nicole." She grabbed Artie the cat from Robyn's arms. "Oh, and did I tell you that Mrs. Marvin said that there was some type of national writing contest and she thought that I should write an essay for the contest based on my editorial in the last newsletter?"

"Cool!" Robyn said, switching Willie from one arm to the other. "I can see the headlines on our next newsletter now: Mack Wins the Pulitzer."

"Ummm. I don't think she meant *that* contest," countered Alex.

"And don't forget," added Amy, "you promised to write an article for my newsletter, too."

"You bet. And Robyn, too," answered Alex.

"What?" Robyn yelled, trying to hear Alex as a large truck rumbled by.

Alex began to reply, but an *"oops!"* from Amy caught her attention. Amy was trying to hold on to Buster as he pulled on the leash, barking and trying his best to attack the truck as it passed by. Amy eventually lost the fight, and Buster ran, full speed, toward the street.

"Buster, no!" yelled Robyn, trying to hold on to the now squirming Willie.

Confused by the yelling and running, Buster suddenly came to a stop, then turned and started running back toward Alex, Robyn, and Amy. As they scattered in all directions, the scared dog headed for the Mack garage.

"Oh, no!" yelled Alex. She handed Artie to Robyn. "I'll go get him." All Alex could think of was Buster knocking over Annie's equipment and papers, something she really didn't want to have to explain to her sister. Alex reached the garage ahead of Amy and Robyn. "Buster!" she called breathlessly, looking around for the dog. The garage seemed very still, and Buster was nowhere in sight. As Alex bent down and checked under the car, she heard a noise behind some boxes at the back of the garage. Slowly, she tiptoed over to the cartons and peered over the top. There was Buster, lying on the floor of the garage, contentedly chewing on something in his paws. "Buster, you should be a detective," she said softly, chuckling.

Amy caught up to Alex and looked over her shoulder at the dog. "Oh, gee. Of all the clumsy—"

"Nope," said Alex, holding up her hand. "Not this time, Amy. Do you realize how long I've been looking for that tennis racket?"

Amy and Alex laughed as Buster contentedly chewed on the wooden racket. "Well, this certainly is a first for me then," replied Amy. "Usually, my clumsiness leads to—well, let's just say, some exciting times."

"I'll say," Alex agreed. "But, hey, Amy, you really did teach me and the others some valuable lessons. I don't think I can thank you enough," said Alex, putting out her hand.

"And you're super, Alex Mack," Amy said, taking Alex's hand.

"Umm. I think I know that one," replied Alex.

"My interpretation is that you're a remarkable person, Alex," added Amy, laughing. "And I can see good things happening to you—good and amazing things."

Alex nodded and smiled. She looked down at Buster, watching him chew, and for a moment, she thought she could see a smile on his face, too.

Dear Theresa,
I guess I was wrong about these American technoids. They really DO know they have it made! I helped my friend's group put together a newsletter, and if I do say so, it was smashing! I'll be home next week. Tell Maurice I expect to see most of the newspaper finished when I get back—with the story of the red squirrel on the front page. See you soon.
Amy H.

Dear Annie,
We ALL won the newsletter contest! And now I know that computers *and* the good old ways both have their place. So you were right, oh brainy one. Things did work out after all! (And I only used you-know-what a few times—but really, really, really, no one but Ray saw me.) Not only that, I bought a new tennis racket (don't ask). . . . I've got to go. The others are going to the new Virtual Reality Center near the mall, but I'm going with Nicole to

hit the ball around the tennis court. I haven't gossiped with Nicole in a while—and I need the break after two weeks as the head honcho of the newsletter! :) . . . Hope you're feeling better, Love (as Amy would say) . . . Love, Alex

About the Author

Patricia Barnes-Svarney writes on a computer most of the day, and daydreams about being one of the first humans on Mars—but will settle for finding a Martian rock on Earth. She writes not only fiction but also nonfiction, and you can often see her name in magazines and along the bindings of science books for young readers and adults. In her spare time, she's either feeding the animals in her backyard, reading, herb gardening, birding, rock hunting, or hiking. She is the author of *Star Trek: The Next Generation: Starfleet Academy: Loyalties*, *Star Trek: Voyager: Starfleet Academy: Quarantine*, and two other *The Secret World of Alex Mack* books—*Junkyard Jitters!* and *High Flyer!*; and is currently working on several science books. She lives with her husband in Endwell, New York.